D0927946

THE LIFELINE

THE LIFELINE

Margaret Mayhew

severn
House

This first world edition published 2020
in Great Britain and the USA by
SEVERN HOUSE PUBLISHERS LTD of
Eardley House, 4 Uxbridge Street, London W8 7SY.
Trade paperback edition first published
in Great Britain and the USA 2020 by
SEVERN HOUSE PUBLISHERS LTD.

British Library Cataloguing in Publication Data
A CIP catalogue record for this title is available from the British Library.

ISBN-13: 978-0-7278-9042-9 (cased)
ISBN-13: 978-1-78029-689-0 (trade paper)
ISBN-13: 978-1-4483-0414-1 (e-book)

All Severn House titles are printed on acid-free paper.

Severn House Publishers support the Forest Stewardship Council™ [FSC™],
the leading international forest certification organisation.
All our titles that are printed on FSC certified paper carry the FSC logo.

MIX
Paper from
responsible sources
FSC
www.fsc.org   FSC® C013056

Typeset by Palimpsest Book Production Ltd.,
Falkirk, Stirlingshire, Scotland.
Printed and bound in Great Britain by
TJ International, Padstow, Cornwall.

To Audrey and Jack

ONE

The committee meeting for the annual Frog End village summer fête was always held in early May, leaving plenty of time for a full discussion of any changes to be made and for any new ideas to be thoroughly aired.

The fête had been held at the Manor for as long as anyone could remember, though during the late Lady Swynford's reign things had not always gone smoothly, due to her many vetoes and quibbles. However, since her unfortunate demise (murder, in fact), her daughter and heir, Ruth, had proved to be as obliging as her mother had been difficult. Last year's fête had been an unqualified success and there was every reason to expect this one to be as good, or even better.

On the sunny morning of this year's committee meeting, the Colonel and his neighbour, Naomi Grimshaw, widowed like himself, walked to the Manor from their respective cottages on the village green. May, he decided, was his favourite month of the year. Naomi, often unpredictable in her opinions, told him that hers was October.

'It's the light, Hugh. Like somebody's changed the bulb to gold. Makes everything look gorgeous.'

That was true enough. But nothing, he thought, could match the arrival of spring after the long, dark months, and May was the high point of that miraculous awakening and the transformation from drab winter to glorious summer. In army postings abroad, he and his wife, Laura, had missed out on English springs and Laura had always dreamed of them retiring to the countryside one day. They had been home on a summer leave, touring Dorset, when they had come across a rose-covered cottage, looking idyllic from across a village green. Years later, after Laura had died, he had found the village, Frog End, and the cottage again, but not looking anything like as idyllic on a cold, wet, winter day. Close-up, the house was dilapidated and forlorn – paint peeling, timbers rotting, thatched roof disintegrating, the rambling rose run wild.

There had been a For Sale sign leaning at a drunken angle by the front gate and he had visited the local agent. The cottage was called Pond Cottage, though there was no sign of a pond, and the price the highest its owner, a local farmer, had had the nerve to ask. Against all sense and reason and in defiance of an appalling survey, he had bought it. The wiring had been a dangerous disgrace, the kitchen range a museum piece, wood and coal were kept in the scullery claw-foot bath, and the lavatory, skulking in an outhouse, was surrounded by a stingingly hostile barrier of nettles.

Builders and painters and thatchers had set to work and Naomi from Pear Tree Cottage next door had given expert advice on tackling the jungle of nettles and brambles at the back, eventually aided by a strong-armed, young gardener, Jacob, seconded temporarily from his work in the Frog End Manor gardens. They had even discovered the lost pond, choked with weeds and covered in green slime that the Colonel had managed to clear out himself. He knew that he could never hope to emulate Naomi's demi-paradise next door – she was a natural-born gardener – but he was making some progress, along with plenty of mistakes.

It had been a wonder to watch the rare and beautiful Three Ships snowdrops that Naomi had given him making an early Christmas appearance under the old lilac tree. They had been followed by the humbler catalogue snowdrops that he had picked more for their nice names than for anything else: Merlin, Wendy's Gold, Magnet, Ophelia, Augustus. Then came the aconites and crocuses and the drifts of daffodils and narcissi that he had also laboriously planted, one by one, and, later still, the bluebells. To his mind they were the most English of all wild spring flowers. Primroses were strong contenders, but the bluebell was the winner. He thought that Laura would have agreed.

Pond Cottage had been his home for three years now and he seemed to have been accepted by the village. As Naomi had once put it – when she had wanted him to do something useful – he was now a respected member of the community, as well as an old soldier, both of which incurred obligations.

He had volunteered his services for various worthy causes – graveyard grass cutting, door-to-door charity collections, driving his old Riley car to and fro on hospital runs, supporting jumble sales and anything that would raise money to keep the village church still standing, with its roof intact. The new young vicar had recruited him as a sidesman and as a lesson reader which he had agreed to, though reluctantly.

Under considerable pressure, he had given a talk in the village hall about his career in the army. It had seemed a poor comparison with other residents' contributions, which were invariably accompanied by impressive slides, but the audience had been appreciative and there had been many questions afterwards.

Major Cuthbertson, a fellow army retiree who lived at Shangri-La, a sensible new-built bungalow, together with his redoubtable wife, had lost no time in passing on the job of treasurer of the fête committee.

'Nothing to it,' the Major had assured him. 'Done it for years. Piece of cake.'

He had soon discovered that it was nothing of the kind. The committee meetings were very long and very tedious, and the day of the fête was spent counting up hundreds of pounds in very small coins. He had also discovered that the Major, a regular at the Dog and Duck pub and whose wife happened to be chairman of the fête committee, was now very happily in charge of the Bottle Stall.

Naomi, striding along beside him in a magenta tracksuit and wearing the huge white trainers that he privately called her moon boots, was giving him some useful gardening tips.

'You can get rid of the old daffodil and tulip leaves now, Hugh. They've had long enough hanging around. Chop 'em down and throw them on the compost heap. The bulbs'll keep in good shape for next spring.'

'Anything else I should be doing?'

'Where's that mint I gave you?'

'Growing in its pot near the pond.'

'Too far away. You'll never use it. And how about getting some other herbs going as well?'

'Such as?'

'Parsley, sage, thyme, rosemary, chives – the basic cooking ones. But plant them right by the back door so they're close at hand. No good having them down the garden or you won't bother with them.'

. He rather doubted that he would anyway. Naomi had made noble efforts to widen his cooking range, writing out simple recipes in her near-illegible scrawl. She was a wonderful gardener, but an erratic speller and he had had some difficulty following her 'Sheperd's Pie' and her 'Tode in the Whole'.

'I don't have room. That bed's full of Ruth's hellebores.'

Ruth had given him the plants last year, dug from the Manor garden, and he had planted them where he could see them easily from the kitchen window. They flowered from Christmas till Easter and beyond. A cheer-up on the gloomiest days.

'You could always move them.'

'They're non-negotiable, Naomi.'

'You sound like Prince Charles being stubborn about Camilla.'

'I'm not budging on the hellebores.'

'All right. Then get a nice old sink from that junkyard where you found the flagstones for the sundowner and use it for your herbs.'

The sundowner terrace at the back of the cottage had been Naomi's brainwave. He had sometimes suspected that the whole idea had been inspired by the prospect of pleasant summer evenings drinking outside, as opposed to inside by his sitting-room log fire.

The six o'clock ritual had started on the very day that he had moved in to Pond Cottage. Naomi had called, or, more accurately walked straight in, and he had invited her to join him in a glass of whisky, which she had accepted with alacrity. Her usual brand, she had informed him, was the current cheapest supermarket offer and, for her, Chivas Regal was a real treat. The ritual had continued ever since. A hefty shot in each glass – neat for him and with a splash of ordinary tap water for her. No ice in either which he thought killed the taste and she considered a waste of space. On that same day, another visitor had entered the cottage uninvited. A mangy, battle-scarred, torn-eared, black and tan cat had turned up and, after inspecting the sitting room and sniffing carefully at the packing boxes, had jumped up on to the sofa, clawed at the cushioning and settled down. The Colonel had clapped his hands threateningly but in vain. The cat had ignored him.

Later, he had discovered that the animal was a stray that had moved into the cottage with the previous tenant, Ben. When the old man had died, the cat had vanished. According to Naomi, Ben had named him Thursday because that was the day when he had first appeared. Since he had also returned on a Thursday to favour Pond Cottage with his presence once more, the Colonel had seen no reason to change it.

Naomi had nagged him about the sundowner terrace until he had, finally, given way. A local reclamation yard had provided beautiful and very expensive old flagstones and Jacob, borrowed once again from the Manor, had laid them. The Colonel had to admit that it had been a great success. The flagstones looked as though they had been there for centuries and it was very pleasant to sit out on a summer evening, watching the sun go down behind the trees, glass in hand and chatting. Naomi would dispense invaluable garden wisdom, and cooking tips – to the benefit of both his garden and his previously non-existent cooking skills – and, in between, she would regale him with village gossip, often fascinating but seldom malicious. Though it was true to say that there had been two murders in the village since the Colonel had moved into Frog End three years ago, as well as one questionably accidental death, the village appeared to be a quiet and orderly place. Beneath its placid surface, however, lay a swirling maelstrom of intrigue and misbehaviour, monitored closely by an undercover network that rivalled the Russian KGB. Naomi had a finger on its pulse.

'Freda Butler dead ahead,' she said, in the manner of a lookout reporting from a ship's crow's nest.

They caught up with the small figure, trotting along in her navy-blue skirt and cardigan, navy-blue hat on her head and navy-blue handbag over one arm. Miss Butler had served in the WRNS until her retirement and she never wore any other colour. Her late father had been an Admiral and she occasionally referred to him in conversation – but not very often. The Colonel had noticed his studio portrait in full dress uniform placed on the top of a bureau in Miss Butler's pin-neat Lupin Cottage, and it was an intimidating sight. She had once confided to him that she had been a sad disappointment to the Admiral, firstly by not being a son, and secondly, because she had not risen to a higher rank in the service. For some reason, people often confided in the Colonel. He had no idea why.

The irony was that quiet, self-effacing, little Miss Butler was one of the founder members of Frog End's crack surveillance team – thanks to her pole position at Lupin Cottage on the edge of the village green and also to a powerful pair of German U-boat commander Zeiss binoculars, rumoured to be stamped with the Nazi swastika. It was generally believed that she had discovered them at the back of the drawer of the old bureau – her sole inheritance from her father – though since the Admiral had only been known to sail a desk during the war, it was a mystery how he had acquired such a prized trophy. Miss Butler, herself, had never spoken of them and kept them hidden out of sight in the bureau drawer, but their existence and deployment at Lupin Cottage's sitting-room front window was common knowledge. Through them, Frog End's peaceful village green was kept under as close scrutiny as the storm-tossed ocean waters had been during the Battle of the Atlantic.

When they drew alongside, the Colonel raised his cap. 'Do you mind if we walk with you, Miss Butler? We all seem to be heading the same way.'

She went a little pink in the face. 'Not at all, Colonel.'

In addition to her navy-blue handbag, she was carrying a spiral-bound reporter's notebook. Among her many village voluntary activities, Freda Butler was secretary of the summer fête committee and in charge of taking the minutes – a task as thankless as his own as treasurer. She had to record everything that was said during the meeting – the impractical proposals, the endless arguments, the hard-fought decisions

– and all in a coherent form that could be read back at the start of the following meeting without giving offence or cause for more argument.

They slowed their pace to Miss Butler's smaller steps, escorting her on each side. Since the Colonel was well over six foot tall, and Naomi Grimshaw shorter though wider, they dwarfed her. She smiled up at them both in turn.

'What lovely weather we're having! Let's hope we're as lucky for the fête.'

Being England, the odds were against it, as they all knew very well. Wet weather contingency plans would have to be made at the committee meeting, involving teas being served in the old stables and some of the more vulnerable stalls, such as cakes and books and bric-a-brac being moved into the house. The late and un-mourned Lady Swynford, Ruth's mother, had refused to allow anything inside beyond the hallway, with all other doors kept firmly locked, but her daughter was another matter.

The Manor had become very different since Ruth had taken over – reverting to the village-friendly place it had been when her father, Sir Alan, had been alive. Ruth had rescued the neglected gardens, abandoning her job in London to work in them herself and thereby discovering an entirely new and unexpected interest. The Manor's old gardener had long since retired and others, much less satisfactory, come and gone, when Jacob had turned up at the Manor some time ago, asking for work. A gangly young man, dressed in shapeless clothes and a floppy hat. Origins unknown, reliability uncertain, inarticulate, clumsy and, it had to be said, more than a bit odd. Ruth had taken a chance when she had hired him but he had proved his worth.

Jacob was not the only good decision that Ruth had made. After a long and unhappy involvement with a married man in her London days, she had finally agreed to marry Tom Harvey, the Frog End village doctor, and the Colonel had been surprised and delighted to be asked to give her away at the church wedding. At the end of April, Alan – named after his late grandfather – had been born.

Miss Butler trotted a little faster. 'I wonder if we shall catch a glimpse of the baby today.'

Naomi grunted. 'Hope not. Children should neither be heard nor seen, in my opinion.'

Naomi described herself as widowed though, to be strictly accurate, she had been divorced from her husband for some years before he had died. In her view, widows had a far better image than divorcees and she chose to ignore the timing. A stingy bastard or a mean old skinflint was the way she usually described her former husband. Their one and only son had emigrated to Australia and married a dyed-in-the-wool sheila who, apparently, hated the English weather. Visits to Pear Tree Cottage were rare and Naomi's two grandchildren were usually referred to as those little Aussie buggers.

Miss Butler was looking rather shocked. 'I'm sure you don't really mean that.'

'Yes, I do. Still, I'll try to make an exception for Ruth.'

They were approaching the gates of the Manor and the driveway that led up to the beautiful old stone house. The wisteria that clambered across its front was in full bloom, bearing heavy bunches of pale mauve flowers. The door had been left open and they went from the bright sunlight into the cool dimness of the oak-panelled hall. The late Lady Swynford's black poodle was there to greet them but without the shrill yaps and pogo stick bouncing that the Colonel remembered from his very first committee meeting. Ruth had re-trained and transformed the creature. Gone was the ridiculous topknot and pom poms clipped like topiary over the shorn body; gone, too, was the brightly jewelled collar. Shoo-Shoo had become a normal dog with a normal coat and normal behaviour. Not the breed of dog that the Colonel would personally have chosen, but perfectly reasonable.

As they entered the large drawing room, where most of the committee members were already assembled, he also remembered how he had felt on that first occasion – rather like a new boy at school. He had been an object of curiosity. Apart from Naomi Grimshaw, Miss Butler and Major Cuthbertson – dumper of the treasurer's job – the rest of them had been strangers to him. Mrs Cuthbertson, the Major's wife, was revealed as Madam Chairman, Mrs Bentley and Mrs Thompson ran the all-important Cake Stall, Mrs Warner was in charge of Bric-a-Brac, Mrs Latimer had Books, Mr Townsend was Hoop-la, Mrs Fox did the teas and Phillipa Rankin, with her weather-beaten cheeks, jodhpurs and jumper stuck about with stray pieces of stable straw, provided the pony rides from her riding school. Now he knew them all.

Ruth had come into the room but without the baby, which would be a disappointment for Miss Butler. He saw how well motherhood suited her and how happy she was looking. Marriage to Tom, the increasing success of her plant-selling business at the Manor and the arrival of young Alan had changed her life. He was very glad for her.

She came over to him. 'Ready for the fray, Hugh?'

He smiled down at her. 'As ready as I'll ever be.'

The committee members were sitting on chairs arranged in a circle round the room and Marjorie Cuthbertson had taken up Madam Chairman's place in front of a small table. She was tapping her pencil sharply to call the meeting to order. Miss Butler cleared her throat and began to read out the minutes of the last meeting.

Surprisingly, there were no quibbles or corrections and they were duly signed. The vicar's fulsome note, apologizing for his unavoidable absence on parish duties, was mentioned but nobody seemed unduly concerned. Tony Morris was a nice and well-meaning young man who had come to Frog End with his guitar and a number of enthusiastic and novel ideas, such as substituting the old wooden church pews for tubular steel stackable chairs to provide space for community activities, and for replacing the ancient flagstones with a new, trip-free, disability-friendly surface. The proposals had fallen on barren village ground, along with his doomed attempt to advance from the old and familiar common prayers to the modern series alternative. The Colonel, a non-believer since his wife's suffering and death, had remained neutral. Attending church was something he still did out of habit and because he enjoyed singing the hymns.

The committee meeting proceeded and the Colonel listened to the inevitable fight over the trestle table allocations, with Mrs Bentley of Cakes insisting that she and Mrs Thompson couldn't possibly manage with less than three and Major Cuthbertson of Bottles objecting to his miserly one.

'Just as popular as your cakes, you know.'

'I think not, Major. Cakes are always the biggest draw by far. And, personally, I don't think we should be encouraging the sale of alcohol at all.'

'We're not selling it. It's a tombola.'

'I'm well aware of that, but it amounts to the same thing.'

The Major went on muttering under his breath, while they moved on to other things. The silver band had been booked, as usual, and could be relied on to work its wavering way through all the old favourites throughout the afternoon: 'Born Free', 'The Dam Busters March', 'Don't Cry for Me Argentina', 'We'll Meet Again' and, if necessary, 'Singin' in the Rain'. Teacups for the teas, or rather the lack of them, were discussed. Mrs Fox took offence.

'Well, it's not my fault. We replaced any missing or broken ones last year. Not with the same pattern, unfortunately. It's no longer available. Mixing china looks slapdash, in my view. Still, people don't seem to care about things like that these days.'

Mrs Warner of Bric-a-Brac spoke up. 'The ice creams were very popular last year. We sold an awful lot of them.'

'Huh! That's easy enough. All you have to do is scoop the stuff out of tubs. My teas are prepared by hand and all the sandwiches and cakes are homemade.'

Mr Townsend intervened quickly. 'Well, I hope we're going to have a duck race again, Madam Chairman. It was a great success, don't you think?'

'It would have been a great deal better if there had been a clear winner. Chaotic is the word that springs to mind.'

'How about a dog show, then? They're always popular, I believe. The most obedient dog, the one most like its owner . . . that sort of thing.'

'I doubt if Mrs Harvey would care to have her gardens invaded by a pack of strange dogs.'

But Ruth didn't mind at all and said so at once.

What a contrast to her late mother, the Colonel thought, remembering Lady Swynford's flat refusal to allow a children's small pet show to be held in a corner of the gardens. Guinea pigs, tortoises, hamsters, goldfish and the like would apparently escape and do untold damage.

After more discussion, the dog show was eventually agreed upon but with the democratic proviso that expensive pedigree breeds were to be excluded.

Mrs Latimer of Books had another idea. 'If I may suggest, Madam Chairman, we could hold a photographic competition. Say, the best photo taken in and around Frog End during the past twelve months. Unframed, four by six inches. Entry one pound and prizes for three different age groups.'

Madam Chairman demurred. 'It would need to be under cover – in case of rain.'

Which led them inevitably on to the wet weather contingency plans. Always a grim subject, though far less so now that Ruth made the house available as an emergency retreat.

The meeting eventually finished with sherry and the Colonel helped Ruth to pass round the glasses.

'Will you stay on for a bit, Hugh? There's something I want to ask you.'

'Of course.'

The Major was still muttering about his one trestle table. 'Damn fool nonsense. That woman and her bloody cakes! It's the same every year and I'm left with nowhere to put my bottles. Serve them right if I resigned.'

The Colonel looked sympathetic. 'I'll change with you, if you like. You could have your job back, as treasurer.'

'No, no, no! Couldn't possibly, old chap. Duty calls and all that.'

So did Madam Chairman, beckoning him imperiously with her pencil. The Major hurried obediently to his wife's side.

As requested, the Colonel waited until the committee members had finished their sherry and gone.

Ruth came straight to the point. 'It's another favour, I'm afraid, Hugh.'

'I'd be glad to help, if I can.'

'Tom and I would like you to be Alan's godfather. Do you think you could bear it?'

He was as taken aback as he had been when he, a relative

newcomer to the village, had been asked to give her away at her wedding.

He said slowly, 'It would be a very great honour, Ruth. But I'm afraid I'd be quite the wrong person.'

'We think you'd be exactly right.'

'The problem is that I don't believe in God.'

'Maybe not, but you know all the ground rules, don't you? And you play by them. That's the important part.'

'I'm also too old.'

'Not so. You'll be around for years yet. Old soldiers never die.'

'But they fade away.'

'Only very slowly. Please say that you will.'

He had taken on two godchildren in the past, reasonably successfully. He knew the general drill. Christmas and birthday presents, useful cheques and cash handouts, visits whenever possible, keeping up with their progress, taking an interest. He also seemed to remember that he had made some serious declarations and promises at both baptisms about their religious education – when he had had some belief of some kind – but which he had failed dismally to keep. It was true, though, that he still followed the general basic rules, or tried to. After all, Jesus of Nazareth had outlined them himself and he was nobody's fool.

He said, 'I really think you should ask someone else.'

'We already have. He needs two godfathers, as well as a godmother. An old friend of Tom's is going to be the other one. We want you to be like an honorary godfather and grandfather combined – if that makes sense. Tom's father and mine are both dead, so you'd be helping us out.'

Tom had got him through the early days at Frog End when he had doubted if life was worth living – dispensing common sense rather than drugs. As for Ruth, she was rated very highly in his book.

He smiled. 'Put like that, it's hard to refuse.'

'Good. That's settled.' She put her arm through his. 'So, come and meet your godson.'

He was asleep upstairs in the Manor nursery – a proper old-fashioned one with a gas fire and a brass-railed guard, an oilcloth-covered table, glass-fronted bookcases, big toy cupboards, and a dappled rocking horse with a flowing mane and tail prancing in the shadows. The Colonel laid a hand on its ears as he passed and it creaked quietly to and fro. He looked down into the cot.

It was many years since his own children, Marcus and Alison, had been born, and he had forgotten how very small new babies were. How vulnerable. Laura had done most of the handling and the hard work. In those days, fathers had played a lesser role, whereas nowadays they seemed to do everything – bathing, nappy changing, pram pushing, bottle feeding, winding. He had seen Marcus in action with his own children, Eric and Edith, taking over from Susan whenever necessary.

When Eric had been born, the Colonel had been guiltily aware of a lack of enthusiasm on his part for his grandson who had inherited his mother's looks – her pale face, gooseberry coloured eyes and wispy hair. It was no help that Susan had encouraged the idea that Eric was a highly-strung and very sensitive child. An expensive consultant psychologist had said so and it was, apparently, important to make all kinds of allowances for temper tantrums, whingeing and whining. The Colonel's fingers had sometimes itched to administer a sound corrective slap.

Aged four, Eric had been sent to stay with him at Pond Cottage while Susan had been in hospital expecting Edith. The Colonel had taken his grandson on a brisk and soldierly tour of the Military Tank Museum at Bovington nearby where Eric had tackled an assault course without hesitation and they had fired guns at targets and generally made a lot of noise. In the museum canteen, and afterwards at the cottage, he had allowed Eric all kinds of hitherto forbidden and unhealthy things to eat – chicken nuggets, beef burgers, chips, frozen peas, tomato ketchup, ice cream, coloured fizzy drinks, bags of popcorn and crisps. He had also let Eric watch Susan-banned TV programmes. A firm male bond had been formed between them, as well as an unspoken pact of silence.

He looked now at this new young person in his life, fast asleep in his cot, and hoped that he could also somehow be of use to him.

On the way down the stairs, Ruth said, 'Actually, there's someone else I'd like you to meet, Hugh. If you could spare the time.'

He braced himself.

'Oh?'

'It's a patient of Tom's. His name's Lawrence Deacon. He and his wife bought one of the flats at the Hall a while ago.'

The Hall had been Naomi's former childhood home in Frog End – a huge, ramshackle, old place that she and her sister had inherited and later sold when it had become impossible for them to maintain. A property developer had bought it for a song and turned it into what he had called deluxe apartments. The Colonel was familiar with them because he had done door-to-door charity collections at the Hall and it had been when he had been rattling a tin for the Save the Donkeys fund that he had discovered the body of a well-known actress in her flat. As Naomi had once tartly observed, he seemed to have developed an unfortunate habit of getting mixed up with dead bodies. Five, all told, counting the two when he had been away from Frog End. It was becoming positively careless.

'I don't think I've met them.'

'You wouldn't have done. They used to live in Dorchester before he retired. The poor man had a stroke soon after they'd moved into the Hall. He was in hospital for a long time until they finally sent him home. Tom's been keeping an eye on him.'

'He's in good hands.'

'Yes, I know. The trouble is recovery is very slow and he's stuck on his own all day long in the flat. Nobody to talk to. Nowhere to go. Nothing to do. Very depressing.'

'It must be. But what about his wife?'

'She works every day in Dorchester. She runs a rather upmarket gift shop there. Her husband needs her, but so does the shop. He's very much at a loose end – if you see what I mean.'

He did. Finding himself alone after a lifetime spent in the company of others had been very hard to get used to. Family, school friends, fellow officers and men, Laura and the children – there had always been someone there, always something happening, always something needing to be done. The terrible silence left had been oppressive, almost audible.

Music had helped, especially playing his old Gilbert and Sullivan records. So did the ritual six o'clock drinks with Naomi. And the various worthy village causes. And, of course, there was always Thursday. But the old stray who had deigned to share Pond Cottage with him wasn't quite the same as a human being, although sometimes he came quite close to it.

'I'm not sure what I could do.'

'Nor am I exactly. Tom's been worried about him. Apparently, he can't see much point to life any longer.'

He knew all about that too.

Ruth went on. 'Then Tom had this idea, you see. He suggested to him that he should come here and do a bit of gardening whenever he felt like it – as much or as little as he wanted. He told him that he could either go on sitting on his backside watching television all day or get out and do something useful instead. Well, he walked over from the Hall and started yesterday.'

'Very good advice. I hope it does the trick.'

'So do I. He's been busy potting up some of the rosemary cuttings that I took last autumn. Rather fiddly for him, but at least he can sit down to do it. Will you give him some encouraging words?'

'I'd be glad to.'

The beneficial effect of gardens and gardening was something that the Colonel could vouch for personally. Before he had moved into Pond Cottage he hadn't been able to tell a daffodil from a daisy, but, thanks to Naomi, he had learned enough to make some order out of the jungle he had so rashly acquired and he had also discovered that there was a good deal of pleasure to be had in the process. Working in a garden was balm to the soul, Naomi had assured him, as well as creative. Hours passed easily. Plants became friends. He had even found himself talking to them, like Prince Charles apparently did. Naomi swore it made all the difference and, as she had pointed out, they answered by growing or not growing. The right plant in the right place was another mantra of hers that he had adopted. You couldn't force a plant to grow where it didn't want to be. Better to move it somewhere else, or cut your losses – like playing poker. Pull out and wait for winning cards.

Tom Harvey's stroke patient was at work in one of the Manor's very old and beautifully dilapidated greenhouses, sitting on a stool in front of a bench and absorbed in transferring a rosemary cutting from its nursery quarters to its more grown-up home. The Colonel could see from his slow and awkward movements that it was a difficult job for him.

Ruth made the introductions and Lawrence Deacon held out his left hand.

'The other one's not much use yet. Glad to meet you, Colonel. Rather slow progress being made here, I'm afraid.'

His speech was slurred and the stroke seemed to have taken its toll on the right side of his face and body. According to Ruth, he had recently retired and so would probably be somewhere in his sixties.

'Well, it looks like you're doing an excellent job.'

'I hope so. I shouldn't like to do any damage.'

Ruth said quickly, 'We're very grateful for the help.'

The Colonel turned to her. 'Naomi has been telling me I should plant some herbs to cook with and she mentioned rosemary. Could I buy one of these?'

'You can have one for nothing, Hugh.'

He smiled. 'That's kind of you, Ruth, but I'd like to pay for it like a proper customer.'

Her plant business was doing deservedly well. Almost everything she sold was grown from scratch, along with any advice needed. The gardening talks given periodically at the Manor by green-fingered people like Naomi were invariably packed out.

'All right. If you insist. I've got some other herbs coming along, if you're interested. Thyme, mint, parsley, tarragon, coriander . . .'

The last two sounded well beyond his cooking range.

'I'll start off with the rosemary.'

Jacob had appeared beyond the greenhouse doorway, poised like a timid wild animal ready to bolt, and Ruth went off to speak to him.

Lawrence Deacon dragged another pot towards him. 'Bit of an odd cove, isn't he?'

'Jacob's a very good gardener.'

'Unlike myself. Dr Harvey thinks this sort of thing will speed up my recovery. I hope he's right.'

'I'm sure he is. Gardening can be very therapeutic. I can speak from experience.'

'I've never done any before and, to tell you the truth, I can't say I'm enjoying it much, but at least it's better than watching daytime television. Have you ever done that, Colonel?'

'No, never.'

'It's a fate worse than death.'

The Colonel remembered visiting an old people's home and seeing the inmates all fast asleep in front of a blaring television set.

'I know what you mean.'

'What made you start gardening, Colonel?'

'Buying a cottage with a jungle attached. Something had to be done.'

'Are you married?'

'My wife died some years ago.'

'Sorry to hear that. Is that why you moved to Frog End?'

'One of the reasons.'

'My wife, Claudia, is thirteen years my junior and will certainly outlive me. It's better that way round, in my opinion.'

'I agree.'

'Us men aren't supposed to be much good at coping alone, are we? Women seem to manage better. Claudia runs a gift shop in Dorchester and I've been finding it hard to get through the days on my own without her. We don't need the money but she seems to need the shop, though I don't understand why.'

'Do you have any children?'

'We had one son but we lost him when he was a teenager. Otherwise, life might have been very different.'

It was the Colonel's turn to express sympathy at what had to be every parent's worst nightmare.

Lawrence Deacon crooked his right arm round another pot to shift it closer.

'We don't talk about him any more. Haven't for years. Claudia has her shop and I used to have my work. Now, I seem to have nothing. There's not much point in looking forward and none at all in looking back.'

'I think you'll find that gardening can help in all sorts of ways.'

'Did it help you get over the loss of your wife?'

'It made it easier to live.'

'I haven't lost my wife yet. But I'm wondering how long she'll stay.'

The Colonel watched another cutting make the trip, shakily but successfully, before he left to walk home. He doubted if anything he had said to Lawrence Deacon had done any good. The man seemed embittered by the hand he had been dealt in life – the death of his young son, his stroke, and the evidently shaky relationship with his wife. It was unlikely that he would find much comfort from re-potting rosemary cuttings.

As he let himself into Pond Cottage, he could hear the phone ringing. When he picked up the receiver in the sitting room he heard his daughter-in-law's voice at the other end of the line. She always spoke loudly as though he were rather deaf.

'Hallo, Father. How are you?'

He had tried, but failed, for several years to get her to call him Hugh.

'Fine, thank you. How are you, Susan?'

'Oh, we've all had dreadful colds and Edith's has gone to her chest. It's been quite worrying. The new doctor refuses to give her an antibiotic.'

'I don't think they like to use them too often.'

'Well, as I said to him, Edith is very delicate. Eric was just the same at that age. His lungs were very susceptible. Fortunately, he seems to be growing out of it, though you can't be too careful with children, can you?'

'No, indeed.'

There was a happy medium, he supposed, between caring too much and not caring enough, between being over-protective and being neglectful. Hard for any mother to gauge, though he thought that Laura had always got it right. Susan's next question was one that he always dreaded.

'When are you coming to see us, Father?'

He was ashamed that he went so rarely. He found the highly polished and pin neat house in Norwich depressing. Susan's health-conscious vegetarian meals verged on the inedible and the lack of alcohol in any form, let alone whisky, was a severe trial.

He said, 'I was hoping you might all come and stay here with me. The cottage is quite civilized now.'

'Not with Edith's chest, Father. I couldn't take the risk. We do worry about you on your own, you know. It would be so much better if you were nearer us.'

He said mildly, 'I'm not on my own. I live in a village with people monitoring my every move.'

'But they're not your kith and kin, are they? It's not the same thing at all.'

He knew what was coming next. His daughter-in-law launched into the attack.

'I happened to hear yesterday of another bungalow near us that's just about to come on the market. All in apple-pie order. No horrid stairs, of course. Gas-fired central heating. Two good-sized bedrooms. Modern bathroom and kitchen. Double glazing to windows. Small, easy-care, paved garden.'

The estate agent's details were obviously close to hand. He waited.

'It would suit you down to the ground, Father. You could view it when you come to stay. It's only round the corner.'

The battle of the bungalows had been going on for some time. He had countered every ploy of Susan's to lure him into buying one in Norwich and abandoning Pond Cottage, which she considered unsafe and unsuitable for someone of his advanced and decrepit age. He knew that she acted from the best of motives but it had to be stopped.

He said gently but firmly, 'I appreciate your concern, Susan, but there's no need for you to worry about me. I like living in Frog End and, as I've mentioned before, I very much dislike bungalows.'

'There are no stairs.'

'I'm aware of that but stairs provide useful exercise. It's good to have them.'

'Oh, well, in that case . . .'

She wouldn't give up, he knew, and time was probably on her side. Instead, she altered course.

'Are you eating properly?'

'Yes, very well.'

'And taking those vitamin pills I told you about?'

He lied without hesitation. 'Of course.'

'It's very important to take good care of yourself.'

'I know.'

'I read an article in the paper saying that Vitamin B is very good for arthritis.'

'Fortunately, I don't have arthritis.'

'A lot of people your age do, Father. It can happen.'

'Yes, I know.'

Pages rustled purposefully.

'I'm just looking at my diary. The best time for you to come and stay with us would be after the summer term ends, otherwise you wouldn't see much of Eric now that he's at school all day.'

'How about a weekend before? I could take him out somewhere.'

He had been planning to take his grandson to one of the old wartime bomber airfields in Norfolk ever since their visit to the Bovington Tank Museum near Frog End had proved so successful. Some of the old runways, control towers and buildings still survived, he knew, and they could have a happy time driving round abandoned perimeter tracks and exploring together. Perhaps even roaring down a potholed runway, pretending to be taking off on a bombing raid. Susan, however, was most unlikely to approve of the idea and the trick would be to slip the leash with Eric on some false pretext. The male bond forged between them among the Bovington tanks would ensure secrecy.

'Not in term time, I'd afraid, Father. He gets much too tired. I have to make sure he gets plenty of rest at weekends.'

'I'll come in the holidays, then.'

'That would be best. I'll think of something nice for us all to do together. We could go to the seaside, perhaps, if the weather's warm enough.'

Sadly, the bomber airfields might have to wait.

He said heartily, 'That sounds like a very good idea.'

The conversation petered out. He replaced the receiver, regretting that his relationship with his well-meaning daughter-in-law was not closer. Laura would have handled things so much better.

Thursday was curled up asleep at the end of the sofa – the end nearest the fireplace, and his place for most of the winter. Now that it was spring, he would probably take a walk in the garden when he woke up. Nothing strenuous. A quiet stroll to survey his territory and check for any unwelcome intruders, with a lengthy pause at the pond to watch the six goldfish who had grown considerably in size since the Colonel had rescued them from a very small glass bowl in a pet shop. He fed them twice a day and they always swam up close to the pond edge. At the last count there had still been six, but they were growing tamer and bolder than was wise for their health and safety, given Thursday's interest.

The challenge of providing a tempting alternative evening meal for the cat lay ahead and it was nowhere as easy as feeding the goldfish. The ritual seldom varied. Whatever the Colonel had bought with high hopes to match the high prices, the old cat would approach his dish with extreme caution and suspicious sniffs. If the Colonel were lucky, he would take a tentative nibble and then settle down to eat; otherwise he would simply walk away. It was anybody's guess how Thursday had acquired his expensive and picky tastes, given his previously precarious existence.

By contrast, the Colonel's own diet was simplicity itself. Naomi had given him easy recipes and he had progressed from not knowing how to boil an egg to converting a few raw ingredients into a passable meal. But he had no real interest in cooking for himself. Naomi's herbs were a nice and kind thought but were likely to remain purely decorative.

TWO

'How's he doing?'

Ruth said, 'Not too badly. He's not really very interested but he gets on with things. It was a good idea of yours, Tom. I just hope it works out for him.'

She doubted that most GPs would take anything like the trouble that Tom took with his patients. He gave them far more than the customary hurried ten minutes. He looked at them rather than at the computer screen; he listened to them and he asked the questions that counted. Apparently, it was often the things that people didn't say that were the most important – the vital bits they left out, let alone the lies they told. The biggest lie was usually about how much they drank. Tom often doubled the amount, sometimes even more, depending on his reading of the patient. He'd learned to judge people very quickly, he said. From the first time they walked into his consulting room, and often before they'd uttered a single word, he knew whether they would tell him lies or the truth. He needed the truth but the lies were understandable. They were born of pride, or shame, or fear. Whatever the reason, the truth had to be coaxed out somehow, if he was to help.

'Lawrence Deacon was giving up, Ruth. Life can get too much for some people – too lonely, too difficult, too sad, too much of a struggle. It comes down to the same thing – they decide they don't want to go on any longer. The only cure is to discover something that gives them a reason to get out of bed in the morning. Gardening can be a very good reason, can't it? You found that out yourself. Nature can be a wonderful healer.'

It was true that after her mother had died so horribly and everything had been so grim, the gardens of her childhood home had miraculously granted her a new lease of life. While she had been away working in London, she had never given them a thought, until she had gone home to care for Mama and noticed how sadly neglected they had become. She had decided to do something about it and the impulse had grown into a passion that had taken over and changed her perspective. She had been able to think more clearly and more objectively. She'd seen what a fool she'd been to waste all those years with a married man who had never had any intention of leaving his wife, and she'd seen what an idiot she'd been not to have appreciated Tom. Luckily, he'd stayed around until she'd finally had the sense to agree to marry him.

She said, 'Well, I've told Lawrence he's only to do as much as he feels like and to stop and go home whenever he wants. I'll keep an eye on him, Tom.'

He put his hands on her shoulders. 'Thank you, Ruth.'

'I'm glad to help. But oughtn't I to pay him?'

'I think that would be a mistake. He might feel obliged to do more than he should or needs to. Let it be strictly voluntary.'

She hesitated. 'The only problem might be Jacob.'

'Why?'

'Well, you know what he's like. Wary of strangers. He won't go near Lawrence, let alone speak to him. I think he's got it into his head that he might be after his job – that he's a threat of some kind. I've tried to explain things, but he doesn't listen.'

'He'll settle down once he gets used to him.'

'I hope so.'

Poor Jacob. Life hadn't treated him kindly. Police investigations into Mama's murder had revealed that he had been abandoned as a baby on the doorstep of a children's home in a cardboard box that had once held packets of Jacob's Cream Crackers – hence his first name. The word Crackers was unfortunate. Tom thought he had probably suffered brain damage at birth as well as emotional trauma. He had spent time in a hospital mental ward and more time wandering homeless, until he had somehow ended up like a lost soul at the Manor. Ruth had offered him a job in the gardens and a place to live in the old stable block. He trusted her, in as much as he trusted anybody, and she felt responsible for him. Mama, of course, had hated his strange ways and wanted to sack him but Ruth had let him stay on. The fact was that now she couldn't manage without him.

Tom said, 'I've got another patient who could do with some gardening therapy as well. Do you think you could cope with a second one?'

'Who is it?'

'Her name's Joyce Reed.'

'I don't think I know her.'

'She's new to Frog End. She and her husband have bought Lois Delaney's old flat at the Hall. She needs some company.'

'How about her husband?'

'She's a golf widow. He's never there.'

'I can't do very much about that, can I?'

'In a way you could. I'm hoping you might be able to take her off my hands occasionally. She's in the surgery almost every day.'

It wasn't at all unusual, she knew, for women of a certain age to fall in love with their doctors, especially if they were doctors like Tom. It had happened several times and it was tricky for him to deal with tactfully but firmly.

She said, 'I don't think gardening will put her off, Tom.'

'I'm not the problem. She's compensating for her golf widowhood by imagining she's ill. Symptoms galore and every test under the sun. A GP's nightmare. There's nothing physic-ally wrong, but she's not satisfied. She needs something else to think about. Something to do.'

'She might hate gardening.'

'I haven't even suggested it to her yet. I wanted to sound you out first. It's a lot to ask, I know, Ruth. You've got more than enough on your plate.'

'She'd probably think her doctor's wife was looking for cheap labour.'

'Yes, she might, but it's worth the risk.'

'You need someone else to talk to her about it, Tom. Somebody completely objective.'

'Any ideas?'

Sitting in his living-room armchair at Shangri-La, *The Times* newspaper held aloft, Major Cuthbertson was wondering whether he could risk a quick one before lunch was ready. Marjorie was still banging away with pots and pans in the kitchen, concocting one of her new recipes, and he could never be quite sure how long it would take. The only certainty was that it would be almost inedible. In the good old days, serving overseas, when they'd had cooks and servants a-plenty, he'd looked forward to meals and enjoyed his food, but those times were gone. Apart from the fact that the old girl couldn't cook for toffee, his teeth were no longer up to the challenge of some of the unidentifiable things that cropped up on his plate. And, whereas in the past there had always been an encouraging tincture or two beforehand, served deferentially from a tray, Marjorie had recently decreed an embargo on lunchtime drinks. He was now expected to do without. No alcohol should cross his lips until the clock on the mantelpiece – bequeathed to them, deliberately he suspected, by his late mother-in-law to spite him from her grave – had chimed its six silly chimes in the evening.

He shook his newspaper till it crackled and turned another page. Yet another name from the past had dropped off the perch. Old Dusty Coleman, it seemed, was no more. They'd written some nice things about him and his medal but, if he remembered correctly, he'd actually been a bit of a bastard. Still, it wasn't done to speak ill of the dead. And they were always 'sadly missed', even if everyone was delighted to see the back of them.

He listened for the clatter of plates which would herald the serving of lunch, but pots and pans were still being banged around on the stove. If he was quick, he might manage one, and quick he had learned to be. He crossed the living room to the cocktail cabinet standing in the corner, lifted the lid and removed bottle and glass in a lightning movement that would have done credit to a fully paid-up member of the Magic Circle. The cabinet, which had been presented to him by the regiment on his retirement, played 'Drink to Me Only with Thine Eyes' loudly whenever the lid was opened but he had cut it off in mid-bar. He poured a hefty tot of Teachers – no need to bother with the soda – and replaced the bottle with scarcely another note being played.

The Major sat down in his chair again and raised the glass. Amazing how the stuff warmed the cockles and stiffened the sinews in two shakes of a lamb's tail. He had read somewhere that whisky was called the old man's friend, and a damned good friend it was too. Never let you down, unlike some things and some people. He drained the glass, hid it behind his chair and picked up his paper, turning to the cricketing columns. Life was looking a whole lot better.

Lunch, when it was finally ready, turned out to be surprisingly eatable. Some kind of minced-up meat and he thought he could taste an onion.

'It's cottage pie,' Marjorie informed him from the opposite end of the dining-room table. 'Rather a success, I think.'

It was a warm, sunny day in May, but the old girl was dressed, as usual, in a thick tweed skirt and woollen twinset. Underneath, so far as he knew, there would also be a thermal vest. The Major had been posted abroad to hot spots for much of his army service and his wife had never re-adjusted to the English climate. Only when the temperature climbed safely above seventy-five degrees did she unearth the tropical kit that she had previously worn abroad. Privately, he thought that tweeds actually suited her better, though he would never have said so.

'I called at the Manor this morning, Roger.'

'Did you, dear?'

'To check on some of the fête arrangements with Ruth. I must say she's always very helpful. Quite a contrast to her late mother.'

Nobody in the village had 'sadly missed' Ursula Swynford, the Major reflected. Her husband, Sir Alan, had been a very decent sort of chap but his wife had been a bit of a bitch, it had to be said. An attractive woman, though. He'd fancied her himself and she'd definitely given him the green light, or at least the amber one. He'd had serious expectations in that direction – until she'd got herself bumped off. In fact, he'd been damned lucky not to get involved. His blood still ran cold at the narrow escape.

He took a gulp of water to wash down an unexpected chunk of something.

'All going well, I trust?'

'Yes. Everything under control.'

'How's Ruth managing with things – the baby and all that?'

He knew nothing about babies – somehow he and Marjorie had missed out on one – but he understood that looking after them could be hard work.

'She seems to be coping.'

'Did you see it?'

'See what?'

'The baby. Girl, isn't it?'

'No, Roger. It's a boy. And he was asleep, so I didn't see him. But I did see Ruth's lame duck in the greenhouse.'

'I didn't know she kept ducks.'

'Not a real one, Roger. Surely you've heard about the chap she's taken under her wing? They must have talked about it in the Dog and Duck? Jolly decent of her, in my view. I'm not sure if I'd have the patience myself.'

He rarely listened to village gossip in the pub – there was too much else to discuss. Serious stuff. Damned politicians making a mess of things, foreigners up to their knavish tricks, country going to the dogs, and so forth.

'Who are you talking about?'

'Tom Harvey's patient, Mr Deacon. He and his wife came to live at the Hall last winter and he had a stroke. Tom thought it would help him recover if he did some light gardening at the Manor, so Ruth's been giving him small jobs to do.'

He thought of Dusty. 'Bit risky, isn't it? The fellow might go and have another one.'

'Tom doesn't think so, according to Ruth. It's like occupational therapy – weaving baskets, making clay pots, all that sort of thing – and it gets him outside into the fresh air.'

The garden of Shangri-La was mercifully small. Crazy paving at the front of the bungalow with a narrow flowerbed on each side of the path leading up to the door; a postage stamp of grass at the back and a few shrubs dotted around. He could cut the grass in a jiffy and the old girl took care of sticking in the bedding plants when needed. Marigolds up the path in summer and some dull-looking things he could never remember the name of in winter. He couldn't see any of it being of much help to recover from anything, but, of course, the gardens at the Manor might be a different matter.

He took another gulp of water to send the chunk finally on its way.

'Well, I hope they know what they're doing.'

'I think they do. It seems a very sensible idea. Ruth told me that Mrs Carberry from the Hall who turned up at the coffee morning today has asked her if she could do a few hours at the Manor sometimes as well. Her husband died last year and it's left her very depressed, poor thing.'

He wondered whether Marjorie would be left very depressed if he were to drop off his perch, like poor old Dusty. Somehow he doubted it.

He'd spotted Mrs Carberry arriving at the village hall. A cut above the rest of the coffee-morning crowd and considerably younger. In her mid-fifties, or thereabouts. Nice figure, well-dressed, decent make-up, long hair. He always liked long hair on a woman. Put him in mind of Delilah with tresses flowing over the pillow and all that – though, come to think of it, it was Samson who'd had the long hair and Delilah who'd wielded the scissors, or the knife, or whatever she'd used to cut him down to size. Lucky chance that she'd be working at the Manor.

'Good-looking woman, I thought.'

'Don't get your hopes up, Roger. She wouldn't be interested.'

He ignored the remark. Just because the old girl hadn't been interested for years, it didn't follow that it was necessarily the same with all other women. By Jove, no! Not where he was concerned. Of course, you had to know how to read the signs. He flattered himself that he'd make a pretty good impression with Mrs Carberry and, in his book, it was always open season on widows.

He said, 'As a matter of fact, I was thinking of calling to see Ruth myself. Wanted to ask her if I could store the bottles for the stall somewhere at the Manor. It's a damned nuisance keeping them here. We haven't got the space.'

'I should have thought you'd welcome their company, Roger.'

He ignored that remark too. Treated it with the disdain it deserved. It wasn't even as though people donated anything decent these days. Bottles of homemade wine brewed-up from everything you could think of – dandelions, peapods, parsnips, nettles, turnip tops – not to mention the British sherry, American Coca Cola, and Lucozade. Lucozade, for God's sake! Might as well be cough medicine. He'd be lucky to get one bottle of spirits among them. Still, it was all in a good cause – whatever the cause was this year – usually the church roof, which was always about to fall down.

He finished the rest of the cottage pie without further trouble and wiped his mouth on his napkin.

'I think I'll take a stroll over there later on this week.'

Marjorie was collecting up plates, clashing them together like cymbals.

'You do that, Roger, but don't say I didn't warn you.'

Tanya Carberry was already regretting her rash conversation with Mrs Harvey at the village coffee morning. She had met her once before, but only exchanged a few words. She knew Dr Harvey, of course, being a patient of his at the Frog End surgery, and he had been extremely kind when Paul had died – taken time to talk to her and done his best to cheer her up. But she hadn't been able to stop crying, even after a year. The depression was terrible. She spent hours each day staring out of the window, seeing nothing and thinking about Paul. He had died so suddenly. One moment he'd been there, in the middle of saying something to her, and the next he'd collapsed on to the floor and was gone. There had been no warning, no clue that anything was wrong with him, no time or chance to say goodbye. Apparently, it had been his heart. Last year they had celebrated their silver wedding anniversary and this year he would have been fifty-eight. They had been planning what they'd do when he retired. Go on a long, luxurious cruise, visit India, drive across America from east to west . . . whatever they felt like, whatever they wanted. Now, none of those things would ever happen.

When they had first moved into the flat, it had seemed such a good idea. With both the children grown-up and living their own lives many miles away in America, it was time to downsize. Time to move into something easier to clean, cheaper to heat and with no garden to worry about. The communal gardens at the Hall were looked after by two men who came regularly with professional machinery. Someone else came to wash the windows and somebody else cleaned the entrance hall and the stairs and corridors and watered the houseplants. She had given up the part-time job she'd never much liked and was enjoying the newfound freedom and leisure. It had all made sense at the time. Now, she hated the place. The flat seemed like a prison and, without Paul, she was in solitary confinement.

The village magazine was delivered monthly through the letterbox. When Paul had been alive they hadn't bothered with village activities or meeting the locals. There had been no need because they had had each other. But, for something to do on another long, lonely day, she had sat down and flipped through the magazine and its announcements and reports and advertisements. The notice about a coffee morning had caught her eye.

9.30 – 11.00
Coffee with Home-Made Cakes in the village hall.
Everyone welcome!

She had made herself get up much earlier than usual, washed her hair, taken time with her make-up and put on a dress and high-heeled shoes, checking everything in the mirror, like she always used to do. Her reflection had surprised her. It had been like bumping into an old acquaintance after a long absence.

The village hall had turned out to be a scruffy sort of place with bare floorboards, a flimsy-looking stage at the far end, tubular chairs and Formica tables. There had been more people than she had expected – thirty or more, mainly women, standing around or sitting at the tables and talking loudly to each other. She needn't have bothered about her appearance because most of them looked as though they were dressed for walking the dog. A large, overbearing woman had come up to her and

informed her in a foghorn voice that her name was Marjorie
Cuthbertson. The smaller man, lagging behind, had been introduced as the Major and was, apparently, her husband. When
his wife had moved away to speak to someone else, he had
nudged her in the ribs with his elbow.

'Don't usually come to these things, you know. Too much
of a hen party. Makes me feel like a fish out of water.'

He had mixed up his metaphors, but she knew what he
meant. Paul would have felt the same.

The Major had conducted her ceremoniously to a trestle table
covered with a white cloth where the coffee and home-made
cakes were being served. He had insisted on paying the one pound
fifty price for hers, flourishing a five-pound note. The proceeds
were, apparently, going towards the cost of new curtains for the
stage. Looking at the old ones, sagging wearily on their hooks,
their replacement was long overdue.

Tanya had not enjoyed the coffee morning. People had kept
watching her, although they pretended not to, and she had
realized that she was an object of pity in their eyes: the lonely,
sad widow. The Major had not helped with his over-the-top
gallantry and it had soon dawned on her that he could easily
become a tiresome nuisance. It was when Mrs Harvey had
finally rescued her from him that the conversation she now
regretted had taken place.

She had known that the Harveys lived at the manor house
in the village and that Ruth Harvey raised garden plants for
sale. When she and Paul had lived in their previous home, she
had quite enjoyed doing the odd bit of gardening, until it had
eventually become too much of a chore. Too many flower beds
with too many weeds and too much grass for Paul to cut when
he had far better things to do. For something to say, she had
asked Mrs Harvey how she coped with the Manor gardens.

Mrs Harvey had smiled. 'I couldn't, without Jacob.'

'Jacob?'

'My mainstay. He turned up at the Manor one day, completely
out of the blue, and he's been working for us ever since. He's
a natural gardener, unlike me. I've had to learn the hard way,
from scratch.'

Mrs Harvey had gone on to explain how she had only begun

to take any interest when she had given up her job in London and come back to the Manor to look after her mother who had been ill. Since her father's death, the gardens had slowly degenerated, and she had decided that she had to do something about it.

'Thanks to Jacob, it's been possible to keep things going. And I have another helper now, as a matter of fact. Lawrence Deacon. He and his wife have a flat at the Hall, so I expect you've come across them?'

'I'm afraid not.'

'He had a stroke a while ago and got very bored and depressed sitting around at home all day, so Tom suggested he might do a bit of gardening at the Manor whenever he felt like it. There's something about gardening that takes you out of yourself. It makes you forget other things, or, not think about them quite so much. I've found that out.'

Tanya had thought about the past year, spent crying and looking out of the window and thinking of Paul who would never come back again. Never, never, never. And she had thought of the empty and silent flat waiting for her and the empty and silent days ahead. And she'd found herself saying to Mrs Harvey, 'I don't know anything about gardening but I wonder if I could possibly come and lend a hand sometimes?'

The Colonel was familiar with the layout of the Hall from previous visits and, most memorably, from the time when he had inadvertently discovered the body of the actress, Lois Delaney, in her flat.

He had been collecting for the Save the Donkeys fund, prevailed upon by Miss Butler who had been let down by the Major feigning flu. It had been snowing hard early in the New Year and he had trudged from door to door in the village, carrying a tin decorated with a picture of a sad-looking donkey with sticking-out bones, laden with a burden bigger than itself. He had also been provided with a tray of donkey face badges and a box of pins.

The Hall had been his last stop. All but one of the flat residents had been very generous to the donkeys but there had been no answer at all from Flat 2 on the ground floor. On his way back down, the caretaker's wife had been waiting for him at the foot of the stairs. She had been very worried about the occupant of Flat 2.

'Miss Delaney, the famous actress,' she had whispered to him. 'Though we're not supposed to tell anybody. She's come here to get away from it all. She likes me to give a bit of a clean and tidy-up for her and I've rung her bell several times today, but she hasn't answered.'

She had a key to the flat, the caretaker's wife had told him, so that she could keep an eye on things if Miss Delaney was ever away. She wasn't away now, though. Her car was outside and you could see it hadn't been moved because it was all covered with snow.

At his suggestion, she had rung the doorbell again and when there was still no answer she had asked him to accompany her inside to check that all was well. All had been far from well. The flat had been in complete darkness, the lights fused. The woman had fetched a torch and the Colonel had come across the body of Lois Delaney when he had shone the beam into a bathroom. She had been lying naked in the bath, electrocuted by the hair dryer submerged beside her.

The flat had been empty for some time after the tragedy. He wondered as he rang the bell if the new owners were aware of its unfortunate history.

Mrs Reed opened the door.

She was well on the wrong side of sixty, he guessed, with grey hair, no make-up that he could detect and unremarkable clothes.

The Colonel introduced himself. He was a relative newcomer to Frog End, he said, but had had time to learn a few of the local ropes and he had called by to see if there was anything he could do to help. In fact, according to Ruth, it was Tom who needed the help with this troubled and troublesome patient.

She had looked him over carefully as he was speaking. Evidently, he must have passed muster because he was invited inside.

The interior had changed completely since he had last seen

it. The silk upholstery and tasselled cushions, the fringed lamps, glass tables, gilt-edged mirrors and silver-framed photographs that he had glimpsed by torchlight before discovering Lois Delaney's body had all vanished. The walls had been repainted in plain white, and the furniture and furnishings were equally muted. The only glitter came from a large illuminated glass display cabinet containing a number of silver trophies which he duly admired.

'My husband's,' Mrs Reed said. 'He won them for golf.'

'He must be very good.'

'Arthur fancies himself as another Tiger Woods but a handicap of twenty isn't much to write home about, is it? What's yours, Colonel?'

'I'm afraid I don't play.'

'Nor do I. The game bores me stiff. We've been married for more than forty years and I've always hoped he'd get tired of golf in the end but it's never happened. He took early retirement so he could play all day and every day. I hardly ever see him. I should be used to it by now, but I'm not. It's getting me down and I'm experiencing a number of health problems.'

'I'm sorry to hear that.'

'Growing older isn't easy, is it, Colonel? I'm finding that out. Things start to go wrong, one after the other. The machine begins to wear out and I'm constantly in pain. The doctor here keeps telling me that there's nothing wrong with me, but I know there is. Arthur doesn't care, of course.'

He said, 'Do you have any family living near?'

'No. Our son lives in London. He's married to a very possessive woman. She's made sure we see as little of him and the grandchildren as possible. I do the odd day trip to town to visit them but Arthur won't go any more. That's the trouble with sons, isn't it? I expect you know the old saying: "Your son is your son till he gets him a wife but your daughter's your daughter for all of her life". I wish I'd had a daughter.'

He thought of his close and enduring relationship with Alison. He'd been lucky.

'May I ask why you came to live in Frog End, Mrs Reed?'

'Arthur fell out with the golf club committee in Hampshire

where we were before and he resigned, so we decided to move. He found another excellent eighteen-hole course not too far from here, so he's very happy.'

'How about you?'

'Well, there's not much to do in Frog End is there?'

'Actually,' he said, 'there's quite a lot.'

He proceeded to tell her all about the jumble sales, the bring-and-buys, the coffee mornings, the lectures with slides, the quiz night at the Dog and Duck, the bridge club, the tapestry circle, the painting and pottery classes, the Ladies' Group and not forgetting the Venture for Retired People. As he did so, he watched her face closing up with boredom. He played his trump card.

'And, of course, there's the Manor. There's always something going on there.'

'The Manor?'

He had her attention now. Manors, Norman castles, ancient abbeys, Roman villas . . . they seldom failed to attract interest.

'It's the big house in the village. Dr Harvey's wife, Ruth, inherited it recently. It's been in her family for several generations.'

'Dr Harvey's never mentioned it to me.'

'No, I don't suppose he would.'

Tom's surgery was a modern brick-built hut without pretensions, like Tom.

'I'm sure Ruth would be happy to show you round, if you'd like to see it, Mrs Reed. It's a very fine old place and the gardens are beautiful. Well worth a look.'

Joyce Reed said unexpectedly, 'My mother was a very keen gardener.'

'So was Ruth's late father.'

'I wasn't interested, myself.'

'Nor was Ruth, but with both her parents gone she hadn't much choice. She's done wonders with the Manor gardens, as well as raising plants to sell. I know she'd always be grateful for a little help if you ever felt like dropping in. To pass the time while your husband's out playing golf. There's nothing better for the mind and body than gardening, I can promise you. It got Ruth through a very bad patch. And, speaking personally, I've found it a lifesaver.'

He waited to see if the seed had fallen on fertile or stony ground. There was a moment's silence before she spoke.

'I'll think about it.'

'It feels a bit chilly in here, Johnny. Would you like me to get you a sweater?'

'No, I wouldn't.'

Sheila Turner's son was sitting hunched up in his wheelchair, going through one of the motorbike magazines from the pile strewn on the floor beside him. They were all the same. Pictures of brutal and ugly machines hurtling across the pages carrying crouched and helmeted figures. She couldn't bear to look at them, or understand how he could. How was it possible when one of them had destroyed his life?

The motorbike obsession had started when Johnny had been ten. He'd bought a model from a toyshop with his saved-up pocket money and taken it everywhere with him – zooming it up and down banisters, across tables and along countertops. *Vroom, vroom. Vroom, vroom.* The first one had been bright shiny red, she remembered. The next had been black, the one after that dark green. He had gone on to spend many hours poring over magazines full of real, full-size bikes. Bikes, bikes. bikes. Never cars. At sixteen he'd worked at the Co-op during the school holidays, filling shelves and putting the money he'd earned into a post office account. At seventeen, he'd told her that he was taking motorbike lessons. He had passed the test first time, and a month before his eighteenth birthday he had ridden home the second-hand machine that he had bought through an advertisement in one of the magazines.

Looking back, Sheila blamed herself entirely. She should have stopped him somehow. Warned him of the terrible dangers. Forbidden the lessons, banished the bike, pleaded with him to give it up. Not that anything would have worked, but she would, at least, have tried. If he'd had a father, things might have been different. There would have been more control – two parents to enforce the rules jointly, with joint strength, not one feeble mother. But Johnny's father was long gone.

He'd walked out soon after Johnny had been born and never been heard of since.

The accident had happened quite soon. Johnny had gone off on the bike without saying where he was going and a few hours later a policeman had come to the door to tell her that he had been taken to hospital. He'd been overtaking a car on a corner and hit an oncoming lorry head-on.

The police had driven her to the hospital and Johnny had been lying unconscious on a bed with curtains drawn around him. She had sat beside him for hours, holding his hand. Later, a doctor had come to tell her that his spine had been injured in the crash. Seriously injured. He was moved to another hospital – one that specialized in such cases – and she had been present when another doctor had broken the news to Johnny that he would never walk again.

From that day onward Johnny had retreated into a dark place of his own, somewhere that she could not reach, however hard she tried. There was no comfort or consolation that she could bring him. Or herself. What had happened had happened and nothing on earth could change it.

She had sold the semi-detached house where they had been living and bought a bungalow in a Dorset village called Frog End, not far from Dorchester. It was in a cul-de-sac called The Close, together with nine other bungalows. It had no character, but nor did it have any stairs, or awkward steps or sills to impede a wheelchair. By the time Johnny eventually came out of hospital, she had made it ready for him.

Dr Harvey visited from his surgery in the village and a district nurse came in daily to help with the lifting and the bathing and the dressing; otherwise she managed on her own. As the hospital doctor had pointed out, Johnny was luckier than many – he still had the use of his upper body and arms. He could sit upright, feed himself, reach things, hold things, move the chair around by rotating the wheels himself with his hands.

When the weather was fine, she would take him outside on to The Close pavement, pushing him along past the other bungalows with fanciful names – Journey's End, The Nook, Tree Tops, Shangri-La – and then on up the slope as far as the village green with its old cottages and view of the Norman church. To begin with she had found it very hard work, but her arms were gradually growing stronger.

She knew that Johnny hated the outings. He hated being wheeled along like a baby, and most especially hated it when people stopped to talk to her over the top of his head, as though he had lost his wits as well as the use of his legs. *How is he today, Mrs Turner? Enjoying the sunshine? Nice to get him out.*

But it seemed to her that anything was better for him than just sitting indoors, staring at the horrible bike magazines or at mindless programmes on television.

'Are you sure you don't want a sweater, dear? It's no trouble to fetch it.'

'I just told you, Mum. I don't need one.'

Once she had tried to tuck a rug around his wasted legs and he had wrenched it off angrily, flung it to the floor and told her never to do that again.

'Well, I'll just go and make us some tea, shall I?'

He turned another page of the magazine without answering.

She went to make the tea and brought it in on a tray – teapot, milk jug, cups and saucers and the kind of cake he had once liked but never touched now. She moved the wheelchair closer to the table and he sat, still looking at the magazine and saying nothing, while she drank her tea and ate a piece of cake that she could hardly swallow.

Things would get better, the district nurse had assured her. It took time for people to adjust to and accept such a traumatic change in their lives.

As far as she could see, all the time in the world would make no difference. No difference at all. Johnny had gone away into the dark place and he would never come back to her again.

THREE

The Colonel struck lucky at the reclamation junkyard. Among the rotting benches, piles of tiles, stacks of bricks, rusty railings and garden gates, he found several ancient stone sinks of various shapes and sizes. The one that appealed to him most was large and round with a hump in the middle.

'It's not a sink,' the reclamation man informed him kindly. 'It's a pig trough. The hump keeps the food round the edges, see, so they can all get a fair look-in, not just the greedy ones. Are you thinking of keeping pigs?'

He explained that, no, he wanted it for growing herbs.

'Very nice,' the man said. 'Mind you, it's heavy. But I can deliver it kerbside for you, if you like.'

The price was agreed and delivery the next day arranged. Pond Cottage actually had no kerbside but the trough would be deposited near the front gate. Beyond that, it would be the Colonel's responsibility. He went by the Manor and found Ruth busy in one of the greenhouses.

'I called on Mrs Reed for you.'

'That was kind of you, Hugh. How did it go?'

'Not a great success. She's going to think about giving you a hand, now and then.'

'Well, it was worth a try. Thank you, Hugh. I've never met her, you know. What's she like?'

'A golf widow with nothing very good to say about her absentee husband but there's a cabinet of his trophies on prominent display. She was definitely interested in seeing the Manor, by the way. Apparently, her mother was a keen gardener. I told her you'd be happy to show her round.'

'Any time. Tom says she thinks she's got a slipped disc at the moment so we'll have to wait while that's sorted out.'

'Let me know if I can do anything more.'

'I will. Thanks.'

He said, 'I was wondering if Jacob could help me with some heavy lifting tomorrow if he has a spare moment?'

'He's being a bit tricky at the moment, Hugh. What are you trying to lift?'

He explained about the pig trough.

'I'm sure he will, as it's you,' Ruth said. 'Which reminds me, I've got some herbs put by. The rosemary you wanted, and some thyme and parsley. Will you take them with you?'

'Only if I pay you for them now.'

'It's a deal.'

She gave him the herb plants, potted up and sitting neatly in a cardboard box.

'Lawrence Deacon did these. He's gradually getting the hang of things. I thought I'd see if he could manage a bit of path sweeping, if he feels up to it. Just to make a change of scene. Potting up can get pretty boring. Did you hear about my other gardening volunteer?'

Naomi must be losing her touch or the village grapevine was wilting.

'No, I hadn't heard.'

'Tanya Carberry from the Hall. A real widow this time, left alone with too much time on her hands. She asked me herself if she could come and do some work in the gardens. She's a patient of Tom's and, of course, he's all for it. In his view, gardening is one of the best medicines there is – far better than any pills.'

'That's more or less what I told Mrs Reed.'

'Let's hope she was paying you attention.'

Ruth put another pot into the box.

'Here's something else for you, Hugh. Not a herb, though, and this one's a present – no arguing. Let me introduce you to Miss Jekyll. A variety of nigella or Love-in-a-mist by its common name. She'll grow to about eighteen inches and have lovely blue flowers. She likes the sun, by the way.'

'I promise I'll do my best to make her feel at home.'

Jacob could be seen in the distance, at work on one of the borders, jerking his scarecrow's arms.

Ruth said, 'I'll go and ask him about the lifting, Hugh. It's better if you stay here.'

The Colonel waited, watching as she talked to Jacob. He was well used to the young man's ways – the painful shyness, the inarticulacy, the oddness – but it looked as though things had become considerably worse. Jacob's back was turned to Ruth like a sulky child, and there seemed to be little or no response.

Ruth returned. 'He says he'll come over in the late afternoon tomorrow.'

'Are you sure that's all right?'

'It is with me, but you might find him a bit difficult. I don't exactly know what the problem is, but I don't think he likes having the patients here. He was bad enough with Lawrence and worse when Tanya turned up. I've explained that they're not proper gardeners – just here to help them feel better – but he doesn't seem to understand. If Mrs Reed decides to join us, heaven knows how he'll react. Tom reckons he'll settle down once he realizes they're not after his job.'

'Very probably.'

'Would you say something to him, if you get the chance, Hugh? He'll listen to you.'

People always seemed to have faith in him doing or saying the right thing. They often confided in him or asked for advice which he rarely felt qualified to give.

As in the case of the plant that Ruth had optimistically entrusted to his care, he promised to do his best.

The pig trough was duly delivered the next day. Returning from his regular stint of churchyard grass cutting, the Colonel discovered it parked outside his front gate. He admired it again. A fine old thing, bearing the scars of use and time. A great many pigs must have grunted and snuffled round it over the years, jostling snouts and trotters for position, the greediest ones frustrated by the hump in the middle.

'Good gracious, Colonel! Whatever is that?'

He had failed to hear Freda Butler's soft-footed approach. She was standing a few feet away, hat on head and handbag over her arm.

'It's a pig trough.'

'Really? How interesting.'

He could see that she was none the wiser. 'I found it at the reclamation yard. They were good enough to deliver it for me.'

'I did happen to notice a truck arrive a while ago.'

She would have observed it closely through the U-boat commander's binoculars, monitored the kerbside delivery and wondered.

'The food stays round the edge, you see, so that they all get a fair chance.'

'Are you going to keep pigs, Colonel?'

He smiled at her. 'No, don't worry, Miss Butler. I'm only going to plant herbs in it. Jacob is coming over later to help me move it into the back garden.'

'Well, it certainly does look very heavy.'

'You must come and see it when it's planted up. It will look better then.'

Her cheeks went a little pink. 'How kind of you, Colonel, I'm sure it will.' She fumbled with the clasp of her handbag. 'As a matter of fact, I called by to ask you something.'

'What was that?'

'I wondered if you would be interested in buying some raffle tickets. It's for such a good cause.'

Miss Butler, as he knew to his cost, supported a number of good causes. He had contributed to them all and had even gone round the village door-to-door with a collecting tin. In addition to Save the Donkeys, he had also turned out to help Save the Gorillas who were apparently teetering on the brink of extinction. Described as gentle giants and pictured swinging from branches and cuddling their babies like humans, they were being hunted by poachers with snares and would soon only exist in zoos. People, he had discovered, reacted unpredictably to door-to-door collections, ranging from smiling welcome and generosity, to hiding behind curtains and sofas. On the whole, the donkeys had done better than the gorillas.

Buying some raffle tickets would be much simpler. He reached for his wallet.

'Of course.'

'It's in aid of the Greenfields Animal Shelter,' Miss Butler told him. 'They do wonderful work, saving abandoned baby animals. Kittens, puppies, rabbits, guinea pigs – all sorts.

People buy them as pets for their children and then they get
tired of looking after them and just leave them somewhere.
Ditches, lay-bys, doorways . . . it's quite shocking. The shelter
takes care of them until they can find them a new home. It
gives them a second chance at life, you see.'

He did see. Another indisputably worthy cause.

Miss Butler had found a book of raffle tickets at the bottom
of her bag and was holding them out to him. He could see a
picture of a sad and frightened kitten. He wondered if Thursday
had ever looked like that; somehow he thought not. He knew
nothing about the cat's previous life, but he did know that
Thursday was a survivor to his claw tips and, like Kipling's
cat, the wildest of all wild animals, had most probably always
preferred to walk by himself. All places would have been alike
to him, until advancing age must have finally made a more
permanent billet seem like a good idea. The only hurdle would
have been finding some soft-hearted mug to take him in. As
the Colonel recalled, Thursday had simply walked uninvited
through the open door of Pond Cottage and made himself at
home.

Miss Butler said enthusiastically, 'The tickets cost one
pound each. There are six tickets in half a book which will
help provide food and warmth for an abandoned animal. A
whole book of twelve tickets will go towards any medicines
and veterinary treatment needed. And, of course, there are the
prizes.'

'Prizes?'

'Yes, indeed. Rather good ones, I thought. First prize is a
week's holiday for two people in a luxury hotel in Barcelona,
Spain.' Her cheeks flushed deeper. 'But, of course, I don't
suppose you would care for that, Colonel.'

'I don't think we need worry about it, Miss Butler. I have
never won anything with a raffle ticket in my life.'

'Nor have I. But one never knows.' She read from the ticket.
'The second prize is a crate of sparkling wine from an English
vineyard. I understand that it's just as good as champagne,
whatever the French say. And the third prize is a hand-woven
willow casket of specially selected sun-ripened fruits.'

'I'll take a whole book,' he said, handing over the money.

'That's most generous of you, Colonel.'

'I'm sure it's a very worthy cause.'

'Indeed it is.' The handbag snapped shut, Miss Butler prepared to move on, then paused.

'I hear dear Ruth has a second volunteer to help her in the gardens now. Mrs Carberry, the widow in Flat 4 at the Hall, you know. She's also a patient of Dr Harvey's, like Mr Deacon. Gardening is becoming quite the new therapy, I understand. It's an inspiring idea, don't you think, Colonel? With Mrs Carberry missing her husband so much and both her children far away in America, I'm sure it will do her a lot of good. It's always better to keep busy, isn't it?'

Miss Butler, as he well knew, was fully occupied. When she was not tracking village activities from the window of Lupin Cottage through her swastika-stamped binoculars, she was attending meetings, taking minutes, delivering parish magazines, collecting for charities, and involved in innumerable other worthy community causes.

She put most other villagers, even the likes of Naomi and Marjorie Cuthbertson, to shame, let alone himself. He did his bit but he was not sure that Miss Butler would approve of the time he spent sitting and listening to records and sometimes just sitting. There was little doubt that she was aware of it. His sitting-room window was directly across the village green from hers and with his curtains drawn back open and the binoculars turned up to maximum she would be able to keep him under close surveillance.

Miss Butler took another step and then stopped again. 'A little bird told me that there may be a third person about to join Mr Deacon and Mrs Carberry at the Manor. Do you know anything about that, Colonel?'

'I'm afraid not.'

'I wondered if it might be the newcomer in Number 2 in the Hall? A Mrs Reed? It was formerly Miss Delaney's flat, of course, as I'm sure you'll remember only too well. What a tragedy that was. Quite shocking.'

Literally as well as figuratively, he thought, remembering the hairdryer in the bath.

'I called on Mrs Reed recently,' he said, volunteering a

crumb of information, though she would probably be well aware of the fact.

'I'm sure the flat is very changed now.'

'Yes, it's quite different.'

'I happened to notice Mrs Reed at Dr Harvey's morning surgery yesterday, though she looked perfectly well. She's often there, apparently. Almost every day. Perhaps Dr Harvey has suggested some gardening therapy for her as well, do you think?'

'It's certainly possible.'

'Did you meet her husband when you called, by any chance?'

'No, he wasn't there.'

'Nobody seems to have seen him, but I understand he plays a great deal of golf.'

'I believe so.'

'A lot of gentlemen do, don't they? I've often wondered why. Apparently, he has a handicap of twenty – whatever that means. I hear he's won a great many silver cups and plates so he must be very good. They're all kept on display in the sitting room. I expect you noticed them when you called?'

It was rather a relief to discover that the Frog End grapevine, far from wilting, was in excellent health. He had obviously not been Mrs Reed's only visitor.

'Yes, they're lit up in a cabinet.'

'Really?'

At that moment, Jacob appeared as silently as Freda Butler had done, and hovered at a safe distance.

'If you'll excuse us, Miss Butler.'

'Oh, of course, Colonel.'

She retreated across the green to Lupin Cottage as he and Jacob began the tricky manoeuvre of getting the pig trough to its new home at the edge of the sundowner terrace. It seemed the perfect place.

He thanked Jacob and, as he had done on other occasions when he had helped him in the cottage jungle, pressed some notes into his hand. This time Jacob refused to take them, backing away and shaking his head. It was wiser, the Colonel judged, not to insist.

Instead, he said, 'I'm very grateful to you for giving me a

hand, Jacob. And I know how much Mrs Harvey appreciates all the work you do in the Manor gardens. She has often told me that she couldn't manage without you.'

'There's others now.'

'But they're not real gardeners like you. They're just passing the time, do you see? Mr Deacon has been very ill and Mrs Carberry has lost her husband. Dr Harvey thought it might make them feel better, that's all. There's nothing whatever for you to worry about, I promise you.'

The young man went off without saying another word, head down, shoulders hunched. It was impossible for the Colonel to tell if he had made any impression on him or not.

'I finished my rounds early, Mrs Turner, so I thought I'd call by and see how Johnny's getting on.'

Dr Harvey was kindness itself. Sheila knew he must be a very busy man, but he somehow found time to visit. She always left him to see Johnny alone because she had realized from the first that it was better like that. Johnny could talk to the doctor about all sorts of things, man-to-man – perhaps even about the dark place. She didn't know what was said because she had never asked Dr Harvey and he had never told her. Doctors were like priests, after all, bound to secrecy with their patients.

She showed him into the sitting room where Johnny was reading one of his bike magazines. As always, she offered him a cup of tea but, as always, he declined it.

'I won't stay long, Mrs Turner. Just a few minutes.'

She went and sat in the kitchen and waited.

It seemed a longer visit than usual, and when Dr Harvey came out of the sitting room he lingered.

'I've just been asking Johnny if he could help us out.'

'Help you out?'

It was impossible to see how.

'Yes. You see, things get very busy in the Manor gardens at this time of the year. Ruth can hardly cope and I don't have much time to spare. I asked Johnny if he could give us a hand sometimes.'

She stared at him. 'But what could he do?'

'There's plenty of odd jobs that need doing, if he wouldn't mind.'

'What did he say?'

'He said he might. And that's rather where you come in, Mrs Turner. You would have to take him over to the Manor and then collect him later. You wouldn't need to stay. Do you think you could manage that?'

She could push the wheelchair from the bungalow as far as the green, all right, though it was a bit of an uphill struggle for the last part. After that she could keep to the edge of the road round the green for the rest of the way to the Manor.

'I could manage it all right. If Johnny agrees.'

He smiled at her. 'See if you can persuade him.'

'He won't listen to me, I'm afraid. That's the very last thing he'd ever do.'

'Then we'll leave it up to him to decide, shall we?'

She saw the doctor out and went into the sitting room.

'Would you like a cup of tea, Johnny?'

He shook his head.

If I don't say a word about Dr Harvey's idea, she thought, he might come round to it in the end. And if he mentions it first, I'll pretend to be against it. She went and made a cup for herself and took it into the sitting room.

Johnny turned another page of his magazine.

'Dr Harvey's asked me to give them a hand at the Manor.'

'Whatever for? I don't see how you can.'

'Because he thinks it would be good for me, that's why. I'm not stupid, Mum.'

'Well, I think it's a very bad idea. Much too tiring. I'm surprised at Dr Harvey for suggesting it. I'll tell him so next time he calls.'

He rounded on her.

'You won't say anything to him, Mum. You'll mind your own bloody business. Just because I can't walk it doesn't mean my mind's gone. I can make my own decisions for myself.'

'Anyway, you'd need me to help you.'

'No, I wouldn't.' He held his arms up, flexing them and clenching his fists. 'My legs don't work but my arms and hands are getting stronger all the time. I can do lots of things and I can wheel myself around anywhere I want to go. I don't need you.'

'I'd have to take you there and back though, wouldn't I?'

'That's all. I can do all the rest on my own, without you. Thanks very much.'

His words wounded while they gave her hope. Hope that he might somehow, some day, leave the dark place.

'Please yourself,' she said with a shrug, 'but you'll never manage it.'

FOUR

Lawrence Deacon looked at his watch again. Claudia was late. Not that it was unusual these days. She seemed to get later and later. The TV evening news had been too boring to watch and he'd finished the newspaper crossword. There was nothing else to do but sit and wait.

Another half hour passed before he heard her key in the lock and she came into the sitting room.

He looked at his watch once more. 'I was getting worried about you.'

'I'm sorry, Lawrence. It's been very busy today. Not that I'm complaining.'

She was very proud of her shop, he knew, although he resented the fact. It was a cut above the usual tourist-tat gift shops. She had good taste and chose the stuff wisely and well – he had to admit that – and she seemed to thrive on hard work, to be full of energy and what used to be called vim. By contrast, he felt and looked like a tired and shambling old man, which was exactly what he had become since the stroke.

Claudia was taking off her jacket and heading for the kitchen. Getting away from him.

He said, 'I spent today sweeping garden paths.'

'That doesn't sound very exciting.'

'It wasn't. Ruth thought it would be a change of scene for me, but I got fed up and came home early.'

'I'm sure she'll think of something else for you to do, if you ask her.'

'I'm not good for much else.' He tried, but failed, to keep the self-pity out of his voice. 'Besides, she's got two more of her husband's patients helping there now.'

'Oh? Who are they?'

'That woman, Mrs Carberry, from the flat upstairs whose husband dropped dead last year, and some sulky young man in a wheelchair. I don't know what's wrong with her, but

I gather the boy smashed himself up riding his motorbike too fast. Broke his spine. He'll never walk again.'

'How very sad.'

'It's not sad at all. It was his own fault. Served him right. And he's lucky to be alive, isn't he? Unlike others.'

He didn't actually mention their son who had not been so lucky. Hadn't uttered his name for years, but the memory of him lay unspoken and unforgotten between them. Their boy had been seventeen and it hadn't been his fault at all.

Claudia turned away. 'I'll go and get on with the supper.'

She was always turning away from him, leaving the room, spending as little time with him as she could.

They'd not only lost a son, he thought, they'd lost a marriage. Neither of them had ever got over the accident, and since his stroke, he'd been difficult to live with, to say the least. Moody and bitter and resentful, if he was honest. He was jealous of the shop. The damned place seemed to take up more and more of her time and attention and there was a new glow about her that he'd noticed recently. The glow of success and fulfilment? Or maybe another man?

She was only fifty-two and still an attractive woman. There was no question of them sleeping together these days – not in his perilous state of health. There hadn't been for some time, in fact. He couldn't remember exactly how long. They'd somehow got out of the habit. It wouldn't be very surprising if some bastard was taking advantage. And if Claudia had a lover she might leave him and he would find himself living alone in this godforsaken place. Christ, it would be unbearable! He'd sooner be dead. Much sooner. He forced himself to calm down; to get a grip. Claudia wasn't that sort of woman. She'd never do a thing like that. Would she?

The Colonel carried the drinks tray out on to the sundowner terrace and Naomi arrived on the dot of six o'clock. It was a fine evening – the first really warm one of the year. Instead of her customary tracksuit, she was wearing the long and voluminous purple kaftan that he remembered had been unearthed last year from the trunk in her attic. It had once belonged to her mother who had brought it back from Turkey.

Like the swallow he had spotted swooping over the garden that morning, the kaftan was a sure harbinger of summer. Where Naomi was concerned, hot weather could lead to a rummage through the attic trunk and the appearance of a variety of lightweight garments of indeterminate age and often exotic origin. Sometimes she brought out her late father's ancient panama hat and stuck it on her thatch of grey hair. She was bareheaded now, but, incongruously, she was still wearing her white moon boots under the kaftan.

She had brought him a jar of home-made jam. 'Hope you like the stuff. Can't stand it myself but it's always useful for bring-and-buys.'

He read the crooked label. Rhubarb Jam. As it happened, he liked rhubarb very much, even the mouth-puckering stew of his boarding school days. 'Thank you, Naomi.'

'So, show me your new herb garden.'

He led her over to make a formal inspection. 'It's actually a pig trough.'

'I can see that, Hugh. And a very nice old one too. What a find!'

'The hump in the middle stops the greedy pigs hogging all the food.'

'Yes, I know that too. I'm a simple country girl, don't forget.'

Not a description he would ever have applied to Naomi.

'I've moved your mint in.'

'It's looking very happy in its new home – rather too happy. Don't let it take over, Hugh. The hump won't stop it like the pigs. It'll rampage everywhere. Now, let's see, what else have you got? Rosemary, thyme, parsley . . . so far, so good. There's plenty of room for more. You could get some sage. Maybe chives, too. All jolly useful everyday herbs.'

His daily cooking had, so far, never included any of them but it would be worth a try, to show willing. He gestured towards the terrace.

'The usual?'

'I don't mind if I do.'

He poured the Chivas Regal – three fingers in each glass with a splash of water added to hers, no ice in either – and they sat down in the old wooden steamer chairs he had also found languishing in a corner of the reclamation yard. Cumbersome but superbly comfortable. Naomi settled herself in, parked her moon boots on the extendable leg rest and raised her glass to him.

'Chin-chin, Hugh. This is the life! We might be on some great liner sailing across the ocean.'

'Just so long as it's not the *Titanic*.'

'Good point. Personally, I'd go for the *Aquitania*. Another lovely old ship – nothing like those floating tower blocks today. My Great Aunt Doris sailed in her in the 1920s and she told me it was the best time she ever had in her entire life. Lolling around in chairs like these, playing jolly deck games, drinking champagne, dining and dancing the night away. And they were actually going somewhere, not just round in circles. A proper voyage. First class, of course. Not quite the same in steerage, I suppose.'

'I doubt it,' the Colonel said drily.

Thursday had appeared from nowhere in his offhand fashion, walking rather stiffly towards them. He gave Naomi a wide berth, fully aware that she was a 'dog person'. On the rare occasions when her two Jack Russells, Mutt and Jeff, accompanied her to Pond Cottage, Thursday and his claws had no problem keeping them at bay.

The cat sat down beside the pig trough and began washing his face methodically with his paws.

'Showing his age a bit more these days,' Naomi remarked.

In fact, Thursday's age was unknown. On the only visit to a veterinary surgery that the Colonel had managed to achieve, the vet, who had been on the receiving end of Thursday's spitting fury, had agreed that it was wiser not attempted again unless absolutely necessary. After a rapid examination, he had judged the cat to be somewhere around sixteen years old, to be in fair shape except for a few missing teeth and a touch of arthritis in his hind legs. The torn ear wasn't worth trying to repair. Thursday would certainly not be entering any cat beauty contests.

'He seems to cope all right.'

'Unlike some of us. You should have been at the May Ladies'

Group meeting last week, Hugh. Not a soul under sixty-five and the speaker forgot to turn up. We were left with just the tea and biscuits.'

The Frog End Ladies' Group met every month to listen to a talk or watch a demonstration on a wide variety of topics: Unusual Foreign Recipes, Constructing Hanging Baskets, Recycling Old Items, Rescuing Hedgehogs. The Colonel had heard all about them and had thanked God many times that men were banned from attending.

Naomi took a swig from her glass. 'They're looking for new speakers. I don't suppose you'd come and give us a talk, Hugh?'

'I'm afraid not.'

'They're getting pretty desperate.'

'They must be. But I really have nothing to talk about.'

'Yes, you do. All the stuff about your time in the army. You could do that again. You were jolly good. We were all ears.'

The slide-less talk that he had been persuaded to give soon after his arrival in Frog End had been the first and the last, so far as he was concerned.

'I'm sorry, Naomi. You'll have to find someone else.'

She acknowledged defeat. 'Oh, well. By the way, what are you up to in your shed these days?'

Naomi did not understand his shed. He had bought it a year ago and Jacob had erected it for him on the place where the old outside privy had once stood. It was a plain and simple structure with a door, two windows and some very useful shelves inside. He had used them for stowing a neat row of glass jars full of nails and screws, nuts and bolts, as well as tins and boxes and bottles containing other oddments he might need. He had put up hooks for hanging garden tools, and there was space for the lawn mower. Most pleasing of all, there was also room for a decent-sized workbench where he had been able to carry out general household repairs and put together a World War Two Matilda tank from a plastic kit. He had also made a German U-boat, a Lancaster bomber and a Hurricane fighter. Last winter he had had an electric cable run out to the shed to provide power, light and warmth and he had turned his hand to some quite serious woodwork. He had so far made a toddler's rocking horse for his granddaughter, Edith, which had been given a mixed reception. Unqualified approval from Edith who had clambered on board straight away, and health and safety doubts from his daughter-in-law, Susan, who had been afraid of her falling off. He was now engaged in making a wooden chessboard for his grandson, Eric. It was fiddly work involving cutting and gluing strips of light and dark wood together to be cut across and then glued again to form the squares. The next step would be sanding the board smooth, the final one adding a border and varnishing. Carving intricate chessmen was beyond him so they would have to be bought ready-made. Not real ivory, of course, but perhaps a passable imitation.

He was looking forward to teaching the game to Eric. If the success of their visit together to Bovington Tank Museum and the subsequent battles fought on the Pond Cottage sitting-room carpet with the Colonel's old tin soldiers were any indication, his grandson would relish the essentially military strategy involved – tactics, manoeuvres, outflanking and encirclement, surprise attack, counter-attack, advance, retreat, capture and surrender. The trick would be to keep his mother, who disapproved of war in any shape or form, in the dark.

Naomi's curiosity had been thoroughly aroused by the shed and she had tried a number of times to get inside – efforts that he had lately managed to thwart by fitting the door with a padlock on the outside as well as a bolt inside, and by hanging makeshift sacking curtains at the windows. He had also hidden the key. Her divorced and late husband, Cecil, had, apparently, also had a shed which she had not understood either. The Colonel was on Cecil's side. A man's shed, after all, was his bolthole from the world. A sacred male sanctuary where he could do just as he pleased without disturbance or comment or argument from anyone – especially not women. That was the whole point of it.

'Nothing much,' he said in answer to her question.

'You must be doing something.'

'Nothing that need worry you, Naomi.'

'You could raise some plants in there.'

'It's not intended to be a greenhouse.'

She sighed. 'I'll never understand men and their sheds.'

'I know that, Naomi.' He changed the subject firmly. 'What news on the Rialto?'

Shylock's Venetian enquiry was perfectly understood. Naomi trotted out the latest Frog End titbit.

'Ruth's taken on another lame duck at the Manor. Tom's suggestion, again. I hope he knows what he's doing.'

'I'm sure he does. Who is it?'

'A young man called Johnny Turner. His mother bought one of The Close bungalows recently. He's stuck in a wheelchair after a motorbike accident. You've probably seen her pushing him around. It's a sad sight.'

He had passed them once in his car – a frail-looking woman struggling with a heavy wheelchair, a fair-haired young man slumped inside. A sad sight indeed.

'Is he likely to recover?'

'Apparently not. Spinal damage. He's only nineteen. Imagine how awful it must be for him, Hugh. To know that you'll never walk again. Never lead a normal life.'

'It must be awful for his mother too.'

'Probably even worse for her, poor woman. The husband pushed off years ago – as husbands do – and she's had to cope with the situation on her own. I gather from Ruth that the boy's in very low spirits and very difficult. Tom thought it might help if he spent some time at the Manor, doing any odd jobs they could find for him. The boy wasn't at all keen at first, nor was the mother. Then Ruth thought of asking him to do some of the watering. Not too difficult to manage from a wheelchair with hosepipes, and a pretty important job in those big greenhouses at this time of the year. She managed to persuade him to take it on.'

If anyone could, he thought, it would be Ruth. She would know just what to say and how to say it.

'I think it's an excellent idea.'

'Let's hope he gets on all right with the other two. They seem to have enough problems of their own without having to cope with a tricky teenager.'

'I've never met Mrs Carberry.'

'A very un-merry widow. Her husband's been dead a year

and she's only just started to come out of her shell. I can't see her cheering up a wheelchair-bound teenager.'

'I'm sure Lawrence Deacon will do what he can to help.'

'Are you, Hugh? I'm not so sure. He strikes me as a real old misery guts. Very sorry for himself.'

'He knows all about tragedy. So does his wife. They lost a son when he was young.'

'I hadn't heard that. How did you find out?'

'He told me. I've no idea exactly what happened or how old their son was, but I would have thought he would feel some sympathy for a young man in a wheelchair.'

'Hmm. Well, Ruth will give the boy something useful to do. She might even get him interested in gardening.'

'Like you did with me?'

'Let's face it, Hugh. It's a lifeline, isn't it?'

'So I keep saying to anyone who'll listen.'

'Well, Adam and Eve had a garden. That must mean something, though luckily we wear clothes these days. By the way, I hear you called on the newest arrivals at the Hall – the Reeds.'

'Who told you?'

'Nobody in particular. The village is clued in, as usual – bar the finer details. But you can tell me more, if you like. I'm all ears.'

'There's nothing to tell.'

'You're being ever so discreet, Hugh. What made you go calling in the first place? It's not like you.'

'I was asked to.'

'By whom?'

'It's confidential.'

'Fair enough. But you can still tell me about the Reeds. I've yet to set eyes on her, or her husband.'

'Why don't you call and see them for yourself?'

'Haven't got time, Hugh. So, spill the beans.'

'There aren't any to spill. I only met Mrs Reed. Her husband was out playing golf.'

'So, how old is she?'

'Somewhere in her sixties, I'd say.'

'Our sort of age, then. Tall, short, fat, thin?'

'Medium height, medium build.'

'You'll have to do better than that. Hair?'

'Grey.'

'Face?'

'Normal.'

'Clothes?'

Naomi's colourful and wildly eccentric wardrobe was impossible not to make an impression, but Mrs Reed's had been virtually unnoticeable.

'I really can't remember.'

'Come on, Hugh.'

'Something beige, I think.'

'You'd make a hopeless police witness. Does she do anything?'

'She's a golf widow. Her husband's retired but he's never at home.'

'Cecil used to pretend to play golf when he wasn't in his shed. So far as I could tell he spent most of the time at the nineteenth, drowning his handicap. The game never appealed to me. Is she a happy golf widow? Some women would be only too pleased to have their husband out from under their feet. Men can be a nuisance after they retire.'

'Mrs Reed didn't give me that impression. She told me she'd always hoped he'd get bored of playing so she'd be able to see more of him.'

'Not much chance of that. It must be depressing to be so dependent on a man. Perhaps she should get a dog?'

'I doubt if it would help.'

'She's forever turning up at Tom's surgeries, you know. Is there anything really wrong with her, or is it all in her golf widow's mind?'

'I've no idea.'

'You're not being very forthcoming, Hugh.'

'I've nothing much to say. Let's talk about something else.'

'All right. What's that flat like now? You can tell me that at least. Any traces of our late actress?'

'None at all.'

'Is it beige, like Mrs Reed's clothes?'

'It's neutral.'

'Flat 2 used to be our dining room, you know, before that developer got his ugly mitts on the Hall. You could never describe it as neutral. A bit of a cavern, I'll admit, but it had some wonderful old panelling. I still wonder what the bastard did with it all. Chopped it up and sold it for firewood, I expect.'

Naomi, as he was aware, had never recovered from having to sell her old family home before it fell down. To distract her, he said, 'There was a glass cabinet full of Mr Reed's silver golfing trophies in the flat. All lit up and very impressive.'

'Men do like their trophies, don't they? Cecil's school swimming cup was always out on display. Well, let's hope we get to meet Mr Reed eventually. Perhaps they'll come to one of the village hall talks.'

'It doesn't seem likely. I told Mrs Reed all about the Frog End activities but I don't think she was very keen.'

'There's an interesting lecture coming up soon at the Manor on Capability Brown. Did you know he designed the gardens of Sherborne Castle?'

'I can't say I did.'

'He worked on over one hundred and seventy gardens across Britain. A very busy man.'

'He must have been.'

'And speaking of gardens, Hugh, it occurs to me that it might help Mrs Reed if she were to do a little gardening therapy at the Manor, along with Lawrence Deacon and Tanya Carberry and the wheelchair boy. It could take her mind off some of her ailments and give poor Tom a break into the bargain. Did you happen to suggest that to her, by any chance?'

'I mentioned it.'

She drained her glass. 'I thought you might have done. What did she say?'

'She's thinking about it.'

He stood up. 'The other half, Naomi?'

'I won't say no.'

She seldom did.

FIVE

In the end, it had been easy. Sheila had stuck to her plan of disapproving of Dr Harvey's idea and the more she did so, the more she could see that Johnny might agree to it, just to upset her. She'd kept saying things like, 'You'd never manage without me.' Or, 'You could fall out of the wheelchair and hurt yourself.' Or, 'I won't let you go there; I forbid it.' He'd turned on her every time and sworn at her but, somehow, she'd kept her head.

Then Mrs Harvey had come to the front door one day and she'd been very nice. 'I do hope you don't mind, Mrs Turner, but I wondered if I could ask Johnny a big favour.'

Sheila had shown her into the stuffy sitting room where Johnny had been staring at one of his bike magazines. At first, she had thought he was going to refuse to speak at all. He had sat, head bent, without a word, while Mrs Harvey had told him about the problem she was having keeping all the young seedlings and plants well-watered in the greenhouses at the Manor and how badly she needed some extra help with it. There were long hosepipes that unwound, so it wasn't heavy work, but it took a lot of time. She would pay him by the hour, she'd said. It would be a godsend if he could come over twice a day, first thing in the morning and again in the early evening, just for the summer months. If that wasn't too much to ask? Could they perhaps give it a try and see how things went?

Sheila had held her breath in the long silence that had followed. At last, Johnny had spoken. Or rather, muttered.

'If you like.'

Of course, she still had to keep on pretending. If Johnny guessed how pleased she really was then he was quite likely to change his mind.

'I don't know how Mrs Harvey can expect you to help her, Johnny. What are you supposed to do?'

He'd turned on her, as usual. 'You heard what she said, Mum. She wants me to water the plants in the greenhouses.'

'From your wheelchair?'

'They've got hosepipes.'

'I still don't see how you could manage it.'

'I can do it all right.'

'We'll have to see about that.'

The very next morning she had pushed him over to the Manor. The first part, along The Close pavement, was quite easy. She went past Journey's End, The Nook, Tree Tops and Shangri-La where Major Cuthbertson peered out of his sitting-room window. She was afraid that he might come out but luckily he didn't. Whenever he talked to them, he always spoke very loudly, as though she was deaf and Johnny an imbecile.

There was a steep bit going up to the green and it was always hard work pushing the chair there, but she'd made it all right. After that, she'd kept to the edge of the road and car drivers slowed down and gave them a wide berth.

The sun had been shining brightly like a good omen as they crunched down the Manor's gravel driveway. She felt a small ray of hope in her heart.

'I'm not sure it's going to work, Tom. He's a very angry young man, isn't he?'

'Life's dealt him a pretty devastating blow.'

'He takes it out on his mother. It's a shame.'

'That's another reason why this could be a good thing, Ruth. It might help them both.'

'I hope so. I'm paying him by the hour. It's not like Lawrence and Tanya. I think Johnny needs to feel it's a proper job. Not something we've asked him to do out of pity.'

'I agree.'

'Actually, I'm very glad of the help with the watering and he's coping rather well. It's amazing how he handles the wheelchair – whizzing up and down the greenhouses. You'd think he'd get all tangled up with the hosepipe but he doesn't and he's very careful with the watering. I was afraid he might flatten the plants.'

'Maybe he'll be good at other things too.'

'One problem is that he's not much good with people. When I introduced him to Lawrence and Tanya it was sticky going.'

'How's he getting on with Jacob?'

'Funnily enough, Jacob doesn't seem to mind him at all. I even saw him giving Johnny a hand with winding up the hosepipe.'

'They're both handicapped, that's why.'

Tanya Carberry had found that she was enjoying the work she'd been given at the Manor. It was quite simple. All she had to do was transfer young greenhouse plants into larger pots before putting them out on long benches where they could stay now that the danger of frost was over. Ruth had shown her exactly how to handle them without disturbing their roots or doing any damage and after a shaky start, she'd got the hang of it.

She'd never heard of some of their names before. She and Paul had always gone for the easy-to-grow, ready-to-plant sort you found in big garden centres – geraniums, petunias, begonias, busy lizzies. Ruth grew those too but she also raised much more unusual kinds.

In fact, everything at the Manor was unusual. There was no shop, as such. The plants for sale were either in the dilapidated old greenhouses or outside on the benches. Customers wandered around as they pleased and when they bought something they paid for it in the old stables where Ruth kept the money in an old Huntley and Palmers biscuit tin. Most of the customers were local but others seemed to have come from quite far afield. The Manor, she realized, was becoming rather well known.

Then there were the talks. They were given in the Manor hall by different people on all sorts of gardening subjects and they always attracted good audiences. She had gone to one herself. Naomi Grimshaw, who often called by to see Ruth, had talked about Letting Plants Move About and it had been rather intriguing. Apparently, in Mrs Grimshaw's garden, plants were left to seed themselves all over the place. Poppies popped up in the middle of box hedging, forget-me-knots drifted about unchecked, erigeron daisies spilled over walls and erupted from cracks, foxgloves appeared wherever they pleased, violets edged their way into the lawn, while bluebells and alchemilla had colonized a nice shady corner of their own. Live and let live, was the motto, even extending to weeds. Herb robert, sweet cicely, cranesbill, rosebay willowherb and teazels were all allowed to stay. Let your garden breathe, Mrs Grimshaw had advised. It didn't do to be too tidy. Judging from the loud applause at the end the audience had thoroughly approved. Paul, who had always hated weeding, would have agreed too.

The days that had dragged by so slowly in the flat now passed quickly. At first, she had eaten her lunchtime sandwiches on her own, wherever she was working, but lately she'd taken to going to the old stables where there was a wooden table and chairs. Ruth was always popping in and out, dealing with customers but sometimes, if she was busy somewhere else, Tanya took the money and gave change from the Huntley and Palmers biscuit tin, and when Ruth had asked her to keep an eye on the baby, Alan, while he was asleep in his pram, she'd been happy to do it.

She felt very sorry for Johnny, and for his mother who pushed him twice a day in the wheelchair from their bungalow on the other side of the village green. She knew that he was also a patient of Dr Harvey's, though it had never been discussed. His job was doing the watering in the greenhouses. He did his work well but he hardly spoke to anyone. She noticed, though, that he sometimes talked to Jacob and, even more surprisingly, that Jacob answered.

Jacob frightened her. Once, when she had been working alone in one of the greenhouses, she had turned round to find him standing by the entrance, watching her. He had scuttled off at once, like a frightened rabbit, though rabbit was the wrong word. Scarecrow would be better. Weirdly dressed, clumsy and strange.

She wasn't sure what she thought of Lawrence Deacon. They had done some potting up together for a while. She had made polite conversation and learned that his wife had a gift shop in Dorchester called Seek and Find.

'It's very successful,' he'd said, but not in a pleased sort of way. Instead, he'd sounded resentful. 'She spends most of her time there.' Then he'd said in a different voice, and with a sideways look at her, 'You're a widow, aren't you? I expect you get lonely, all on your own.'

A warning bell had rung. Some men believed, quite mistakenly, that widows were grateful for their interest, but surely not someone like Lawrence Deacon? Not at his age and with his poor state of health?

The idea repelled her. She'd turned away from him. 'I'm used to it now,' she'd said.

Ruth said, 'You've been doing a marvellous job, Johnny.'

He muttered something she couldn't hear and stuffed the money she'd given him in his pocket.

'I was wondering,' she went on, 'whether you might be able to spare us some extra time for a while? There's a lot of box hedging that needs clipping.'

'I don't know how to do that.'

'Oh, it's quite simple. You can use hand clippers and the hedges are only about three feet high and easy to reach.' She paused. 'Of course, it would only make sense if you could stay with us for the whole day – but perhaps that would be too much for you?'

'No, it wouldn't.'

'What about your mother?'

'What about her?'

'She might not think it was a very good idea.'

'It's not for her to say. I'll do it if you want.'

She smiled at him. 'Thank you, Johnny. I'm very grateful. If you brought something for lunch, you could eat it in here in the stables. Mrs Carberry usually does that and I'm always coming in and out to see to customers, so it's all quite busy. You might enjoy it.'

'I'd get in people's way.'

'No, you wouldn't. There's plenty of room for us all.' She smiled at him again. 'So, that's settled, then.'

'Are you sure, Johnny?'

'Why wouldn't I be?'

'I just thought you might find it a bit tiring.'

'Stop treating me like a child, Mum. I know what I can and can't do. And Mrs Harvey needs extra help.'

One part of Sheila was thrilled for him, the other part afraid. The watering had been going well, so far as she could tell – though he never talked about it – but to spend the whole day at the Manor might be a different matter. It could go all wrong, instead of all right, and the door that had opened for Johnny might slam shut again.

'Mrs Harvey? I'm Joyce Reed. Your husband's patient. They told me I might find you here.'

Alan's golf widow was standing at the entrance to the stables. The one who, according to Hugh, was thinking about doing a little gardening therapy. Ruth wondered if she had reached any decision.

'How nice to meet you, Mrs Reed. Can I help you with anything?'

'If you have time, I'd like to see the gardens.'

'I'm free at the moment so I can show you round.'

She gave her the grand tour – the lawns, the herbaceous borders, the rose garden, the pool garden, the lavender beds, the fig walk, the kitchen gardens, the greenhouses, the orchard. On the way they passed Lawrence, Tanya and Johnny at work. Jacob, of course, had made himself invisible.

Ruth said, 'I hope you and your husband have settled into your flat, Mrs Reed.'

'We're finding our feet.'

'It takes time, of course.'

'My health isn't very good, unfortunately.'

'I'm sure my husband will do everything he can to help.'

'Who were those people? That man and woman and the young man in the wheelchair?'

'They're patients of my husband, Mrs Reed, like yourself. They come and work in the gardens whenever they feel like it. I would have introduced them to you, but they were rather busy. Would you be interested in joining them?'

'I have a bad back.'

'We could find some very light work that might suit you.

And perhaps your husband would be interested, if he's retired?'

'My husband isn't interested in anything except golf, Mrs Harvey.'

'I met your golf widow today, Tom. She called by to see the gardens. At least that's what she said, but I think she just wanted something to do. She's probably lonely.'

'So are a lot of people, unfortunately.'

'I suggested she might join the volunteers but her back is still a problem, apparently.'

'Only in her mind.'

'Anyway, I've thought of the very job for her if it does get any better.'

'What's that?'

'Dead-heading the roses. It would keep her busy for the rest of the summer.'

Word of the golf widow had reached the Major's ears via the bar in the Dog and Duck. He had been airing his views on the prime minister's shortcomings, to general agreement, and the conversation had turned to the latest arrivals at the Hall who had moved into Flat 2.

The Major knew all about the flat. Lois Delaney had lived there, and though he had never actually seen inside it, he could imagine how it must have looked when occupied by a famous actress. A glamorous stage set. Nothing less would do for the beautiful woman he had seen act many times in his far-off youth. He'd become a devoted fan and something of a stage-door Johnny, always going round to wait for her to come out after a show. Once, he'd given her a bunch of red roses and she'd given him a wonderful smile in return. She'd actually spoken to him. He could never remember what she had said, but it had been something jolly nice. Tragic the way a woman like that had come to such a sticky end.

Anyway, apparently, some people called Reed had now moved into the flat. The talk was that the husband played a great deal of golf while the wife was left to her own devices.

The Major had pricked up his ears. Widows of any description were of interest and the golf kind might be worth investigation. In general, the widows of Frog End fell sadly short of his benchmark. Mrs Carberry was an encouraging exception, of course, but it was always a sound idea to hedge one's bets.

It seemed that the Colonel had already called on the newcomers, though, which was annoying. Trying to steal a march most probably. Damned unfair, in fact. The Colonel had all the advantages – rank, height, more hair and no Marjorie. The only thing to do was to pop round himself and find out the score. After all, people still called on new arrivals these days, though not like in the old days when it had been a whole palaver of silver trays and cards.

He took some trouble with his appearance – best blazer and regimental tie, handkerchief arranged perfectly in pocket, the remains of his hair carefully smoothed into place, a generous splash of aftershave. When all was said and done, he reckoned he could still hold his own.

In his mind, he pictured how the golf widow might look. Not in the first flush, obviously. A mature woman. But they could be damned attractive in his view. What's more, they knew a thing or two. As he walked up the driveway to the Hall, he built up an image of Mrs Reed. Not too tall, he hoped. On the slim side and with decent legs for a change. Marjorie had legs like the Shangri-La gate posts that she had scraped many times with the Escort. Actually, he was an ankle man himself. Always had been. They were the most important part, so far as he was concerned. The rest didn't matter so much. If the ankles were good he sat up and took notice.

He quickened his pace. The luxury apartments at the Hall had cost a bob or two, so she was bound to be well-dressed, even elegant, and with a cad of a husband who neglected her. Definitely promising.

He had expected to run the gauntlet of a caretaker at the front door but his luck was in because it had been left ajar. Flat 2 was easy to find. He paused to adjust his tie and smooth his hair again before he rang the bell.

The woman who opened the door was grey-haired, dowdy and so far from the image in his mind that he thought she must be someone else. A companion, perhaps – if such a thing existed any more? A housekeeper?

'Is Mrs Reed at home?'

'I am Mrs Reed.'

She looked at least ten years older than he had expected. His expectations had been shattered, but there was nothing for it but to carry on. To bow and smile with all the charm he could muster.

'I'm Major Cuthbertson.'

He had been passing by, he explained, and would like to welcome her and her husband to Frog End. He held out his hand. She took it without enthusiasm.

'You'd better come inside.'

He did so reluctantly but with some dregs of hope. At the very least, she might offer him a drink?

He followed her into the sitting room and found himself blinking at a large and brightly illuminated display cabinet, full of well-polished silver cups and plates.

'My husband's trophies,' she said. 'He's a golfer. Out playing golf, as usual.'

He cleared his throat. 'Well, I hope you'll both like Frog End. Not a bad sort of place, once you get to know it.'

He was invited to sit down on an uncomfortable chair and took a look round. Dreary sort of room, he thought. No resemblance to any stage set he'd ever seen unless it was for some modern rubbish and no sign of any sort of a drink anywhere. Nothing to oil the wheels, as it were. Mrs Reed was watching him closely, waiting for him to say something. He fell back on a safe subject.

'Warm weather we're having.'

She didn't think so. It was rather cold in her view. At least she and Marjorie would agree on that, if they ever met. He searched desperately for another topic but before he could find one, she spoke again.

'I appreciate your calling, Major. I have very few visitors. It can be quite lonely here, you know. I spend a great deal of time on my own.'

He clutched at the chair arm. Was she tipping him the wink? Giving him the nod? Surely not! Not at her age and looking like she did.

'Good idea to get out more,' he blustered. 'Lots going on in the village. I'll get my wife to fill you in.'

'I didn't realize you were married, Major.'

'Rather!' How many years was it? He'd forgotten but it seemed like forever. 'Marjorie will soon have you doing things.'

'As a matter of fact, Mrs Harvey at the Manor has asked if I would consider lending her a hand in the gardens occasionally – on a voluntary basis.'

'Splendid! Just the sort of thing.'

'The trouble is my health's not up to it, and I have a bad back.'

'She'd give you something easy to do. Never say die, Mrs Reed.'

'I don't,' she said. 'And my name's Joyce.'

She poured him a thimbleful of sweet cream sherry which he hated but it would have been rude to refuse. It was another half hour before he could make a decent escape. At any moment he had expected the husband to return and demand to know what the hell he was doing there. Golfers, he knew, were very good at taking a swing at things.

'Come and see me again, Major. Any time.'

'Rather!'

As the door closed behind him, he mopped his brow with his immaculate handkerchief. Damned tricky situation! He'd pass the word on to the old girl about finding the woman something useful to do and he'd make himself very scarce in future. No offence, but the Colonel was more than welcome to her. And she'd had hideous ankles.

SIX

The baptism of Alan Henry Harvey took place in Frog End village church at the end of May. The Colonel had not attended many baptisms during his life but he had always found them a moving experience. There was a small gathering round the invariably ancient font of parents, grandparents, uncles, aunts, cousins and friends, together with the all-important godparents, who were there to make solemn promises on behalf of the infant who was to be admitted to a rather special lifelong club.

'Dost thou, in the name of this Child, renounce the devil and all his works, the vain pomp and glory of the world, with all covetous desires of the same . . .'

He had no problem with any of that and his godson, dressed in a very handsome long lace family robe, seemed perfectly happy about the proceedings. The Colonel watched as Tony Morris, the nice young vicar, who had fortunately left his guitar behind and whose modern, innovative ideas about replacing the church's pews and flagstones, as well as the service words, had been forgiven, if not forgotten, trickled water carefully over Alan's forehead and signed it with a cross.

'. . . In token that hereafter he shall not be ashamed to confess the faith of Christ crucified and manfully to fight under his banner, against sin, the world and the devil; and to continue Christ's faithful soldier and servant until his life's end.'

Stirring words, the Colonel thought, whether you believed in them or not, and spoken in one of the most expressive and beautiful languages on earth.

After the service they trooped outside and stood in the sunshine. Photographs were taken of the Colonel and his fellow godfather on each side of the godmother who cradled their godson expertly.

After a moment, the godmother said to him. 'It's your turn now.'

He found himself left holding the baby. He had made some promises that he could and would keep for the child and some that he could not. He hoped that Ruth had been right about the ground rules being the most important.

She came over to the rescue. 'I'll take him now, Hugh. And thank you.'

'There's nothing to thank me for.'

'Yes, there is. Whatever you said to Mrs Reed did the trick. She's finally decided to join us for one day a week. She's going to be dead-heading roses. Nice and easy. Tom thinks it will help her.'

'I'm sure it will.'

'Apparently, the Major called on her too. I can't think why but he'd better watch out for the golfing husband.'

Tanya Carberry was eating her lunchtime sandwich in the old stables. Ruth had been there for a while, dealing with a customer and now she had gone off again, wheeling Alan away in his pram. It was nice having the baby around. He was very little trouble, unlike her own who had been exhausting – always crying, always wanting something, always difficult. She hadn't enjoyed motherhood at any stage and it had been a secret relief when the children had grown up and left home. She and Paul had been alone together again, which they had guiltily enjoyed.

She thought that Ruth's baby looked a lot like his father, and it occurred to her suddenly that if ever she had a grandson, he might look like Paul, and what a wonderful thing that would be. But neither of her children was married, or even living with anyone, and they were so far away that she would hardly ever see a grandchild. After Paul had died, people had told her that she ought to move to America to be near the children, but the idea of leaving England was unthinkable.

She was halfway through the sandwich when Johnny wheeled himself into the stables. He didn't see her at first, and when he did, he started to wheel himself out again.

She called after him. 'Come and join me, Johnny. I could do with some company.'

'I'll be in your way.'

'No, you won't.' She patted the tabletop. 'There's lots of room.'

He hesitated, hands over the chair's wheels, and then propelled himself slowly towards the far end of the table.

His sandwiches were very neatly wrapped in cling film and foil – undoubtedly the work of his devoted mother. Tanya had watched Mrs Turner when she brought Johnny in the mornings and when she came to collect him later and she had seen how much she cared about her son, how hard she tried not to fuss over him and how angry it made him if she did.

'Those look good, Johnny. What are they?'

'Cheese and tomato.'

'With pickle?'

He nodded and started eating in silence.

I must do better, she thought. Make an effort. Only I'm so out of practice.

'How are you getting on with the hedges?'

'All right.'

'Mrs Harvey told me that you're better than all right. She said you've got a gardener's eye. I know I don't have one but she puts up with me. She's very kind. So is Dr Harvey, don't you think?'

'He's all right.'

'Only all right?'

'He does his best. It's Mr Deacon who's a real bastard.'

'What do you mean?'

'He's horrible to Jacob. He makes fun of him as though he's a complete moron, which he isn't. Jacob's just different and he knows a whole lot more about gardening than the rest of us.'

'So I've noticed.'

'Mr Deacon will get at me, too, whenever he can – telling me I'm doing everything wrong when I know I'm doing it right. I wish he'd go home and die.'

Shocked, she said, 'You don't really mean that, Johnny.'

'Yes, I do.'

It had been a motorbike accident, she knew. Ruth had explained to her briefly. One moment Johnny had been a strong and healthy young man with a boundless future, the next he'd become a wheelchair cripple, his life in ruins. No wonder he behaved as he did. And the Manor gardens, nice as they were, couldn't be much help or comfort.

Another customer came into the stables, carrying a plant. 'Can I pay you for this?'

Tanya said, inspired, 'Could you possibly deal with it, Johnny? I'm in the middle of eating my sandwich.'

For a moment, she thought he would refuse. Then she watched as he wheeled himself over to the biscuit box, took the money and gave change. The customer, like so many of them, wanted advice. Shade or sun? A lot or a little water? Would it need pruning? Feeding? Protection from frost?

To her amazement, Johnny had the answers. He gave them without any grace, let alone a smile, but he gave them and, what's more, they sounded convincing.

When the customer had gone off satisfied, she asked, 'How did you know all that?'

'I listen to Mrs Harvey and I watch what she does, and what Jacob does. I might as well learn something while I'm here.'

'I think that's very sensible of you, Johnny.'

'Well, I don't have much choice, do I?'

'Yes, you do,' she said. 'So do I. We're in the same boat. We can give up on life or we can make something of what we've got left.'

What a prig I sound, she thought. I wouldn't blame him for taking himself off.

He didn't, though. He stayed and finished his sandwiches and when another customer came in he went over again to take the money and give change from the biscuit tin.

'Did you have a good day, Johnny, dear?'

He shrugged. 'All right.'

'What did you do?'

'The usual. Watering, clipping, hoeing.'

The hoeing was something new, but, of course, hoes had long handles so Johnny would be able to reach from the wheelchair.

'Hoeing must have made a nice change.'

'It's boring.'

Sheila set off down the Manor driveway. Pushing the chair gave her blisters but she'd found an old pair of cotton gloves to wear which made things better.

'Mrs Harvey says you're a great help to her.'

'Don't be stupid, Mum. How can I be?'

'She meant it.'

'No, she didn't. She's just sorry for me.'

They went on down the driveway in silence.

After a moment, he said, 'Some woman started asking me a lot of questions today.'

'What sort of questions?'

'She'd bought a plant. She wanted to know how to look after it.'

'Mrs Harvey would have told her.'

'She wasn't there.'

'So, what did you do?'

'I told her myself.'

'You mean you knew?'

'I've still got eyes and ears. And a brain.'

'What kind of plant was it?'

'A pelargonium.'

The ray of hope was back. Only a glimmer, but it seemed that Johnny's days at the Manor gardens weren't just spent watering and clipping and hoeing, as she had thought. He was learning things. Taking an interest. It didn't matter what it was so long as it led him out of the dark place.

'I wouldn't know anything about pelargoniums.'

'Mrs Harvey propagates them from cuttings.'

'How clever of her.'

'Anyone could do it. She cuts off a stem with leaves but no flowers, sticks it in compost and keeps it watered and it grows into a new plant. They come in different colours.'

'I'd like to buy one, if that's all right.'

'I'll pick you one out tomorrow, if you want.'

A bit later, he said, 'There's another patient of Dr Harvey's working in the gardens now, so there's four of us.'

'Who's that?'

'I don't know her name. She's old and she's only coming
once a week for a few hours, so she won't be much use. We've
all got something wrong with us.'

She wanted to tell him that there was nothing wrong with
him except for his damaged spine. That he was getting stronger
every day and that he was going to learn to live his life again,
if only he would give himself the chance. But she didn't dare.

The Major watched them go by from his sitting-room window.
Poor woman, heaving that heavy wheelchair along and coping
with that ungrateful son of hers. Understandable that the boy
got fed up with the way things were, of course, but he should
treat his mother better. Show her some respect. His own mother
would never have put up with it. Nor would Marjorie, if they'd
ever had any children.

He'd stopped to have a chat with the Turners several times
– tried to cheer things up, put in a bracing word or two, but
the boy never answered or even looked up. Damned rude really.
And the mother always seemed as though she'd much sooner
he didn't bother. Fair enough. He could take a hint. Still, it
was depressing to see them going past.

This time, though, things seemed a bit different. The Major
moved closer to the window, peering round the curtain. Mrs
Turner was bending forward to speak to her son over his
shoulder and he had actually turned his head to answer her.
By Jove, for once, he wasn't scowling! That was a turn up for
the books.

His late mother-in law's clock chimed its six silly pings on
the mantelpiece behind him, which meant it was time for a
legitimate pick-me-up. She was another woman who had
always ruled the roost. His late father-in-law, he recalled,
had been no match for his wife, or for his daughter either,
poor chap. Henpecked to the end. The Major sighed. One thing
he'd enjoyed most about the army was that the whole show
had been run by men for men. No messing around with this
modern nonsense of women having a say in everything, let
alone going anywhere near the front line. Men had been left
in peace to get on with a man's job. He fingered his shoulder
that had once proudly borne a major's crown. When he thought

about it, life had never been quite the same since those good old days.

He walked with firm and righteous tread towards the cocktail cabinet in the corner. It had become something of a Mecca during his retirement and, as usual, it started on 'Drink to Me Only with Thine Eyes' the second he lifted the lid. On this occasion, he let it go on playing, his conscience perfectly clear. No need to worry about Marjorie. She was out at one of her interminable committee meetings and, even if she came back unexpectedly early, he had her mother's clock as an unimpeachable witness. He poured himself a large Teachers with a small splash of soda, closed the lid on the confounded racket, and returned to his armchair, raising his glass in a silent toast to himself.

The golf widow had been a big disappointment but, thank God, he'd managed to escape unscathed from her clutches. He'd give her a wide berth in future; avoid her like the plague. He rather fancied his chances with Mrs Carberry now. Since the coffee morning, he'd run across her again at a village hall talk. A weird chap had shown slides about Bird Watching on the Tibetan Plateau, wherever that was. He wouldn't have gone to the talk at all if he hadn't been dragooned by Marjorie into unstacking and restacking the damned chairs. Still, in this case, it had given him the chance of a few more words with Tanya, as he called her now – at least to himself. After that, they had met at the Latimers' annual drinks party, and at Sunday Matins she had been sitting only two rows behind. He had managed to speak to her outside the church afterwards and he could tell that she'd taken note of him. If he said it himself, he was one of the few men in Frog End who had kept his figure and a lot of his hair too. The Colonel had more hair, it must be admitted, and he was taller and a bit younger, but he still carried a torch for his late wife, which rather put him out of the running. The field was clear. It was just a question of how to play it.

He stroked his chin thoughtfully. The fête was coming up before long and he was already collecting bottles for the stall – the usual sort of rubbish that people unloaded on to him which had to be kept somewhere. Whatever Marjorie had said, it was a jolly good idea of his to ask Ruth if she'd let him park bottles at the Manor. Plenty of spare room there, whereas you couldn't swing a cat in Shangri-La. Not a real cat, of course, but one of those things they used for flogging people on ships in the old days. A cat-'o-nine-tails. Nine knotted cords down a rope, flaying the flesh off backs. Life on those sailing ships had been rough. Oh, yes, indeed. Tanya, as he well knew, was helping out at the Manor. He raised his glass again. He'd call by there tomorrow. It was a good idea. A very good idea indeed.

For once, Claudia was home early. When Lawrence heard her key in the lock, he picked up the newspaper and pretended to be reading it and to be very surprised when she came into the room.

'Did the shop catch fire?'

'No, Lawrence, it didn't.'

'Well, you're early. I thought something drastic must have happened.'

'It was an unusually quiet day, as a matter of fact. There was no need for me to stay.'

'I don't see why you ever do anyway. It's your shop. You can just lock up and leave whenever you want.'

'I value my customers. The shop couldn't exist without them, and they keep coming back because I take time and trouble with them. Extra time, if necessary.'

'Far more than you ever do with me.'

'You're not alone all day, Lawrence. You go to the Manor.'

'Ruth's taken on another patient. It's getting too crowded.'

'Who is it?'

'Some woman. She's a golf widow and a hypochondriac. I'm not sure which comes first. All she does is deadhead the roses very slowly. Snooty type. I didn't take to her at all.'

'Well, Tanya Carberry seems very nice.'

'She's all right. But that crippled boy makes me think of what happened to Richard.'

'We agreed never to talk about that again.'

'He reminds me of it whenever I see him. He doesn't deserve to be alive while Richard's dead. I'd like to see him suffer.'

'Don't you think he's suffering already?'

'Not enough. He's been getting quite cocky lately. Zooming about in his wheelchair, like he was still on a motorbike. He should be taught a lesson.'

She turned away. 'That's enough Lawrence. I don't want to discuss it.'

He said. 'Wait. Before you go, Claudia, I want to ask you something.'

She paused reluctantly.

'Yes?'

'I've had an idea,' he said. 'I'd like us to go away for a few days together – maybe to Paris. Remember when we went there years ago, soon after we were married? We could afford a decent hotel now. Have a good time. I don't like the French but I like France. What do you think?'

'I think it would be too risky for you, Lawrence. It's too soon.'

He said bitterly, 'Soon it'll be too late. I'll take the risk, if you will. Shut up the bloody shop, for Christ's sake, and let's go.'

'I can't do that. It's the holiday season – the busiest time of the year.'

'You could, if you wanted to. But you don't, do you?'

'No,' she said. 'Since you ask me, I don't.'

Well, he had his answer. There was someone else, as he'd suspected. That was why she couldn't stand the idea of going away with him. She had a lover. She didn't want him any more and she didn't need him any more. And the sooner he was dead and gone, the happier she would be.

SEVEN

The Colonel was pleased with the progress of his pig trough herb garden. The mint, parsley, rosemary and thyme were all flourishing. He had used some of the mint on Jersey new potatoes, stuck sprigs of rosemary into a lamb chop and scattered parsley and thyme over an omelette. He was ready, he felt, to add other varieties recommended by Naomi – such as sage and chives. On his way back from a shopping trip into Dorchester, he stopped the Riley outside the Manor.

Ruth was usually to be found somewhere in the gardens or greenhouses or stables but this time he drew a blank. Lawrence Deacon, a tray of young plants beside him, was working on a flower bed.

The Colonel paused. 'Can I give you a hand?'

Deacon held out the trowel. 'Here you are.'

The Colonel took over, digging holes, putting in the new plants, firming the soil back in place.

'What am I planting?'

'No idea. Annuals of some sort. I'm not really interested. I just do whatever Ruth tells me.'

Gardening didn't seem to be working any of its customary magic on Deacon, but at least it was getting him out of doors and keeping him occupied.

'I gather Mrs Reed has joined you now.'

'One day a week, that's all. I don't know why Ruth took her on. She's always going on about her bad back or something else she imagines she's got wrong with her.'

'How are you feeling?'

'Worse, if anything.'

'That's a pity.'

'My wife is having an affair, which doesn't help.'

The Colonel stopped planting. 'Are you sure?'

'The signs are there.'

'Signs?'

'You'd know them. You're a man of the world.'

He wasn't sure that the description applied to him in any way.

He said, 'You could be mistaken.'

'Oh, I don't think so. She's been coming home later and later, always making excuses about being so busy at her shop. And there's a different look about her. I can tell she's had enough of me. I'm surplus to requirements now. When I had the stroke, she was very patient at first, but that's all changed. Mind you, I'm a difficult bastard these days, so I can't say I blame her. We used to be happy but the truth is things were never the same after we lost our son. We never got over it, either of us.'

'I'm sorry.'

Deacon said, 'I suggested we went away together – to Paris, like we did once years ago – but she refused. It would be too risky for me, she said, and she can't leave the shop because of the holiday season, but the real reason is that she doesn't want to go with me. She admitted it when I asked her.'

'I'm sorry,' he said again.

'If Claudia leaves me for someone else, I'm finished. She knows that, but I don't think it will stop her. Not any more. She's a lot younger than me with plenty of living ahead. I stand in her way.'

The Colonel resumed his planting. He had never met Mrs Deacon but it seemed to him that her husband was letting his imagination take over. The effects of a stroke were likely to be far-reaching – not just physical but also emotional. A battle on two fronts that Laurence Deacon appeared to be losing.

The Major struck while the iron was hot. It never did, he knew, to shilly-shally once your mind was made up. Straight unto the breach, was his motto, same as Henry V's. Or close the wall up with our English dead! Sounded a bit dramatic, in this case, but it was the general idea.

He strode over to the Manor and banged the knocker on the front door. The only response was the poodle yapping. Useless thing, in his opinion. Any self-respecting burglar would simply kick it aside on the toe of his boot.

After a moment, he walked round the side of the house towards the big lawn and saw the barmy chap, Jacob, trimming the edges. No help to be had there either. Then, as luck would have it, he caught sight of Mrs Carberry herself in the distance, snipping away at something that was growing up a wall. He walked over casually.

'Hallo, there.'

'Hallo, Major. What are you doing here?'

She was definitely pleased to see him, he was sure of it. Not rushing things, exactly, but then she wasn't that sort of woman.

'Actually, I'm after Mrs Harvey. Any idea where she might be?'

'She's over in the stables.'

'Jolly good.' He watched her snip some more. 'You seem very busy.'

'Ruth asked me to tidy this up.'

Whatever it was had grown to the top of the wall and was waving its arms around, looking for somewhere to go.

'Like to do a bit of gardening myself, now and again.'

'Really?'

He thought of the postage-stamp lawn at Shangri-La and Marjorie's serried ranks of marigolds.

'Nothing like here, of course.' He cleared his throat. 'Settling down in Frog End, then?'

She did some more snipping. 'People are very kind.'

'Been to the Dog and Duck yet?'

'I'm afraid not.'

'Not a bad place. Care to join me for a drink there sometime?'

'That's kind of you, Major, but I don't enjoy pubs.'

She was playing it safe, he realized. Quite right too. In a place like Frog End you had to watch your step. A hotbed of gossip, if ever there was one. He'd follow her lead. Another idea came to him out of the blue. Freda Butler was forever trying to get him to collect for one of her confounded good causes: helping the homeless, rescuing mistreated donkeys, saving dancing bears and all that sort of thing. The latest had been in aid of some dodgy animal shelter and she'd

flogged him a bunch of raffle tickets for it. He'd bought them
just to get rid of her, without even bothering to look at the
prizes. Now, if he offered to help her sell some more he
would have the perfect excuse to call at all the Hall flats.
Tanya, as he had discovered, lived in one of them on the first
floor. He could see himself ringing her bell, pretending to
be surprised when she opened the door, proffering the animal
shelter raffle tickets and accepting her smiling invitation to
step inside.

At the moment, though, she was still snipping away, and
her back was still turned. Still playing it safe.

'Well, I'll be getting along, then.'

He found Ruth in the stables and she was jolly decent about
storing the bottles, as he'd known she would be. He could put
them in one of the old loose boxes, she said. So, the scene
was set for him to drop by the Manor whenever he wanted.
On the way home, he called at Lavender Cottage. Freda Butler
was delighted with his offer to help sell the raffle tickets –
astonished, in fact. She unloaded rather more on him than he'd
actually intended, but if they did the trick with Tanya it would
be worth it.

Later on, he read about the prizes. The sparkling English
wine would be rubbish, and he didn't care about the hand-
woven willow casket of sun-ripened fruits, but the week's
holiday for two in a luxury hotel in Barcelona, Spain was
another matter. By Jove, supposing he won first prize with
one of his tickets! The old girl wouldn't care to go to Spain
– too many Spanish – but Tanya might leap at the chance. Or,
better still, what if he happened to sell Tanya the winning
ticket? She'd be bound to ask him along, wouldn't she? Of
course, they'd have to keep it a secret. Cover their tracks, as
it were. He'd spin some story about visiting an old army friend
– Jumbo Buckland, say, if he hadn't already popped his clogs.
You never knew these days.

Johnny was waiting for her, holding a potted plant in his lap.

'This is for you, Mum.'

'For me?'

'Well, you said you wanted a pelargonium, didn't you?'

She stared at the plant with its bright pink flowers. 'It's beautiful, Johnny. How much do I owe Mrs Harvey?'

'Nothing. I paid for it out of my wages. It's called Lara Starshine, by the way.'

'That's a lovely name.'

'It's scented and goes on flowering till December. You could put it in a bigger pot and it'll grow to about a foot tall.'

She couldn't speak for a moment. Her throat had gone tight and she could feel tears welling up. She swallowed hard. It would never do to get upset. Johnny hated tears more than anything.

At last, she said, 'Thank you, Johnny. It's very kind of you.'

He hunched his shoulders dismissively. 'Can we go home now?'

Claudia Deacon put her key in the flat door and opened it. Silence, as usual. No sound of the radio or the television, just a heavy and reproachful silence. She went into the sitting room and, as usual, Lawrence was sitting in his chair, doing nothing.

'You're late again,' he said. He looked at his watch. 'Very late, in fact.'

'I've been very busy today.'

'You always say that.'

'Because it's often true.' She put a heavy supermarket bag down. 'And I had to go and get some food for supper too. You should be pleased the shop's doing well, Lawrence. Would you sooner it didn't? That it failed?'

'I'd sooner you came home on time. You're supposed to shut at half past five, aren't you?' He checked his watch again. 'It's twenty minutes past seven.'

Don't get angry, she told herself. It won't help. Just try to explain, once again.

'I can't just shut the shop and walk away, Lawrence. There are always things to be seen to. A shop doesn't just run itself and it all takes time.'

'So there's none left for me?'

'That's not so.'

'Oh yes, it is. I hardly see you. You'd sooner the stroke had killed me off properly, wouldn't you? Then you'd be free to

find someone else young and fit – not an old cripple like me.
If you haven't done so already.'

She said wearily, 'There's no one else, Lawrence. We've
had this conversation before, and I'm getting rather tired
of it.'

'Like you're tired of me?'

'I soon will be, if you don't stop being so unreasonable.
You're still going to the Manor, aren't you? I thought that was
working quite well. Helping you to get stronger.'

'It bores me to tears, if you want to know.'

'Surely it's better than sitting here all day?'

'I wouldn't mind, if you were here too.'

'I'm not going to give up the shop, Lawrence, if that's what
you're asking me to do.'

'You might have to – if I don't get better.'

There was silence.

She picked up the bag of shopping. 'I'll cook the supper.'

While she was in the kitchen, chopping and slicing and
stirring, she kept repeating to herself, 'I won't give it up,
whatever he says and whatever happens. I won't. I won't. I
damn well won't! I'm not going to let him take away the life
I've earned for myself.'

Ruth found Johnny hoeing in the kitchen garden. She watched
him for a moment, seeing how deft he'd become. He was
learning so fast and doing so well that she was coming to
rely on him almost as much as she relied on Jacob. She went
closer.

'I wondered if you'd like to borrow this, Johnny?'

She handed him the book on gardening. It was an old copy
that had once belonged to her father and which she had used
as a bible when she had taken over the Manor. A simple,
illustrated guide to trees and shrubs and plants – their Latin
and English names, their type, their height and spread, their
colours, their season, their habits, their needs; the basic facts
for any gardener starting out.

'You might find it helpful if customers ask questions.'

He turned the pages slowly.

She said, 'You can let me have it back when you've had

time to look through it. There's no rush. And I've got lots more gardening books, if you're interested.'

She left him with the book on his lap, still turning the pages.

The talk on Capability Brown at the Manor was a big success. The Colonel had been standing at the back of the packed room, listening to the story of one of England's greatest landscape gardeners. Born in Northumberland and christened Lancelot, he had begun his working life at Stowe under William Kent, founder of the new English style gardening. At twenty-six he was already a master gardener and soon became the must-have landscape designer for aristocrats with huge estates. After Stowe came Warwick Castle, Blenheim Palace, Burghley House, Hampton Court, Chatsworth . . . The Capability nickname had grown from his habit of telling his clients that their estates had great 'capability' for improving the landscape. The excellent slides shown gave the proof.

Naomi joined him at the end. 'What a guy!'

She was draped in the impressive purple kaftan recently emerged on its summer outing from her attic trunk.

He said, 'I've been wondering what the great man might have made of Pond Cottage. Do you think he could think very small?'

'I think he could think any size, but the big ones paid the most. There was a downside to some of the grand schemes, though, you know. The big money didn't like little villages spoiling their new view. They thought nothing of doing away with Frog Ends, if they got in the way. Wiped them off the map – church, manor, pub, cottages and all. I see Mrs Reed is here.'

'So she is.'

Joyce Reed was sitting on her own, he noted, at the very front.

Naomi said, 'I finally met her here the other day when she was working at a snail's pace on the roses. I couldn't quite make her out, Hugh. An odd woman. Where's her husband?'

'On the golf course, I imagine.'

'I wonder what he looks like.'

'I've no idea.'

'Wasn't there a photo of him with all the trophies?'

'Not as far as I remember.'

The Colonel's path crossed Mrs Reed's later on as he was leaving the Manor. She was quite enjoying deadheading the roses, she told him, but it made her hands ache. She wouldn't be surprised if she was getting arthritis.

He had known others with that affliction. 'I hope not.'

'I've learnt to take the rough with the smooth, Colonel. One can't always pick and choose in life. If I could, I would prefer not to have Mr Deacon as a fellow worker.'

He was surprised by her remark. 'Has he offended you in some way?'

'In several ways. He gets a lot of pleasure from offending others. But I choose to ignore him. He's nothing, you see, though he'd like to be. In my book, he doesn't count.'

EIGHT

The Frog End summer fête was a big success and voted one of the best ever. The weather had been more than kind – not a cloud in the sky, let alone a raindrop – and attendance figures had been up, as well as the takings.

The Colonel, counting coins and notes at his treasurer's post in the Manor study, sensed a new record in the making. The church roof would be safe for another year.

He had opened the window wide and could hear the silver band working through its customary repertoire with a new addition from 'The Sound of Music' – the familiar tune about the hills being alive. Rather too familiar for his liking. He remembered reading somewhere that the United States Army had once devised a new and subtle form of torture for their more recalcitrant military prisoners by playing them a recording of that very song on a continuous loop for days and nights on end. No rack or thumbscrew had been necessary, apparently. The prisoners were soon ready to talk and cooperate with anything if only the music would stop.

The dog show had attracted a large turnout and the Dog Most Like Its Owner had proved a very popular category. It was won by Mrs Warner who had temporarily deserted her bric-a-brac stall to take part with her spaniel. The old dog waddling alongside her certainly bore an uncanny resemblance.

Ruth had come in with a cup of tea for him and stayed to chat for a while. His godson was apparently sleeping soundly up in the nursery, undisturbed by the band or even the periodic fortissimo megaphone announcements from Marjorie Cuthbertson.

He asked Ruth how the gardening therapy was going.

'I don't think Lawrence is enjoying it much but Tanya seems a lot happier and there's definitely some real progress with Johnny. He's managing incredibly well.'

'That's very good news.'

'Yes, it is, isn't it? I lent him one of my gardening books to take home in the hope that he might take a peek at it and his mother said he read it from cover to cover. Usually he just stares at motorbike magazines. I'll keep on lending the books.'

They could turn out to be a lifeline for the young man, the Colonel thought, and for his mother.

'How about Mrs Reed?'

'I'm not sure how long she'll last. She's working her way very slowly through the roses. For a while she was convinced that she was developing arthritis in her hands but Tom managed to reassure her that she wasn't.'

The band had returned refreshed from a tea break and launched into a spirited rendition of 'The Dam Busters' march. It reached the Colonel through the open study window as he was counting another pile of coins and he stopped to listen. It was impossible not to be stirred by the image conjured up of daring young men flying mighty Lancasters at tree-top height across enemy territory by night.

On guard at the Bottle Stall, the Major was wondering if he dared take a nip from the flask he had brought with him for medicinal emergencies. You never knew when someone was going to faint from the heat, or from anything else. He didn't feel too bright himself, as a matter of fact. Standing killed his feet and he wished he'd had the foresight to pinch one of the chairs from Teas when the harridan who was in charge wasn't looking.

There had been the usual fight over the trestle tables with Cakes which had left him with one miserly table. His bottles were crammed together so you couldn't see the damn things properly – not that there was anything worth seeing or winning. He'd lost count of the grimy bottles of homemade wine that people had foisted on to him, handing the stuff over as though it were five-star Veuve Clicquot.

He decided to risk a quick swig from the flask for the sake of his feet and ducked down behind the stall out of sight. When he emerged, wiping his mouth, some woman was standing there, holding out her tombola money and glaring at him.

He kept a good lookout for the golf widow during the afternoon, ready to duck down again if she turned up. He had spotted Tanya once or twice but she hadn't come near his stall so far. There was such a thing as playing it too safe in his opinion.

It had to be said, the Major admitted to himself, that his plan with the raffle tickets had not gone as smoothly as he had hoped. When he had rung the bell at Tanya's flat at the Hall, she had opened the door but instead of inviting him smilingly inside, as he had hoped, she had left him standing there while she went to fetch her purse. And as soon as she had given him the money and he had handed over the raffle tickets, she had immediately shut the door again – not in his face exactly but very close to it. Even worse, only one of the other occupants at the Hall had been interested in the confounded animal shelter and he had ended up buying the rest of the tickets himself. Miss Butler had been quite overwhelmed by his generosity.

His back-up plan of ferrying the fête bottles over to store at the Manor had not borne fruit either. Whenever he had managed to track Tanya down in the gardens she had been too busy to stop whatever she was doing to talk to him – though he'd spotted her chatting to the Turner boy in his wheelchair several times. All in all, he was beginning to ask himself if she was worth the trouble. There were other fish in the sea, though not so many these days, it was true. On balance, it was probably worth hanging on. Sticking to his course. Playing the game. But now that the fête was over, he must think up another excuse for calling at the Manor.

The new idea came to him later that evening when the fête was over at long last and he was pouring himself a reviver. It was Marjorie's birthday soon, though God knows how old she was now. He'd stopped counting long ago. All women liked flowers – he'd learned that useful lesson very early on in life – and Marjorie was no exception, though he didn't very often remember to get them for her. He'd noticed some good-looking plants flowering away in pots at the Manor. He'd pop by and buy her one as a present. Ruth would keep it there for him until the day. She was always a good sport.

*   *   *

The Major was easy enough to cope with, Tanya had found. He might be a bit of a nuisance but he meant no harm. Lawrence Deacon was another matter. He seemed convinced his wife was having an affair and had tried to talk to her about it. She had stopped the conversation immediately. He wanted her sympathy and she felt unable to give it or to encourage him in any way. She had seen how he treated both Johnny and Jacob and had not been impressed. In fact, he disgusted her. Once, he had deliberately let his hand brush against her. After that she had kept a safe distance away from him.

He had always repelled her physically. Now, she found herself disliking everything about him. She had seen the mocking way that he had treated poor Jacob and how spiteful he had been to Johnny, criticising his valiant efforts in his wheelchair.

Not only did she dislike Lawrence Deacon, she was afraid of him. There was something dark and disturbing about him.

But Lawrence was the only thing she didn't like about the Manor. Everything else was good. The terrible depression was finally lifting. No more long and lonely days in the flat. She now went to the Manor almost every day. There was always something to do, someone to talk to, something happening. She was starting to live again. She wasn't going to let him stand in her way and spoil her chance of a new life. Not now.

'Did you have a nice day, Johnny?'

'Nothing special.'

But Sheila could tell from the way he looked and spoke that the day had gone well, and she saw, also, that he had another book on his lap. One of the gardening books that Mrs Harvey kept on lending him. He didn't talk about the books, but he read them all. When she went into the sitting room these days she'd find him deep in the latest one, studying the pages – the pile of hateful motorbike magazines left untouched. He had even let her see one or two of the pictures and told her the names of plants when she'd asked. He was learning a lot about them. What kind they were, when they flowered, where they liked to grow, how to look after them – all sorts of interesting things.

She pushed the wheelchair down the Manor drive, round the edge of the village green and down towards The Close. The Major looked out of the front window of Shangri La and waved. Johnny waved back. He did that quite often now.

The pelargonium that he had given her was in its glory. She'd bought a big blue glazed pot for it and stood it outside the bungalow front door where it seemed very happy. It made her happy, too, to see it there as they went in and out, just as it gladdened her heart and soul to see the way that Johnny was coming back to her from his dark place. It was like a miracle.

She began to dare to think about a future and she had a plan. She would learn to drive and when she had passed the driving test she would take out some of her savings to buy a car. A car with room for a special folding wheelchair. She had seen them in Dorchester when she had gone in on the bus and had watched people using them. The wheelchair could fold up and fit away in the car boot and then unfold when you lifted it out. And off you went. Easy! She would be able to take Johnny wherever he wanted. A whole new world would open up for him. She had looked in the phone book and found the name of a driving school called Never Fail which sounded very encouraging. But it would be better not to say anything to Johnny yet, she decided. She would keep it as a surprise.

She bought a road atlas in WHSmith and started to look at what they could do and where they might go in Dorset. The sea wasn't far away. They would be able to drive to Weymouth on a green road to look at the beach, even if they couldn't actually get down on it with the wheelchair. Then they would go past Portland Bay where there was a castle, marked in small red letters, and down to Portland Bill to see the light-house. There was a museum and shipwreck centre marked in red too. Johnny would be bound to like those.

Afterwards they could drive west along the yellow coast road by Chesil Beach and on to Abbotsbury, Burton Bradstock and Bridport. She'd never been to any of them but they were nice names and she could see that in some places a yellow road went very close to the sea.

She followed a bendy red road further west, tracing it with

her finger, and it led her to Exeter in Devon. After that, a yellow road went all the way across the middle of Dartmoor. Beyond that was Cornwall. Cornwall! It would be like travelling to a foreign country.

Once she'd done the driving lessons and passed the test, she'd tell Johnny and they could look at the map together and he could choose where he'd like to go. She'd take him anywhere he wanted. Anywhere. Till then, she'd keep it a secret. Hug it to herself and dream.

Then one day, without any warning, everything changed. From light to darkness. From hope to despair.

She'd gone to collect Johnny from the Manor as usual and she could see at once that he was in a very bad mood – hunched down in the wheelchair, head turned away.

'Is everything all right, Johnny?'

'Don't ask stupid questions, Mum. It'll never be all right. You know that.'

She pushed the wheelchair down the drive in silence. Experience had taught her that it was always best to keep quiet when he was like this.

As they reached the gates, he said suddenly, 'Mr Deacon was preaching at me today.'

'What did he say?'

'Rubbish as usual.'

'You mustn't take any notice of him, Johnny. He's not a very nice man.'

'He's a bloody bastard! Do you know, he's glad I'll be spending the rest of my life in a wheelchair. That's what he said to me, Mum, if you really want to know. Glad! He gets a kick out of seeing me like this, being pushed everywhere like a baby. He told me his son had been killed riding on the back of a motorbike and the bloke driving it had got off scot-free when he ought to have been smashed up and crippled for life, like me.'

She stopped the chair, shocked. 'It's wicked to say such terrible things. I'll speak to Mrs Harvey.'

'No, you won't. Don't you dare interfere, Mum. I can look after myself. I've told you that before. I'll get my own back on him, don't you worry.'

When they passed Shangri-La, the Major waved his glass from the window. Johnny took no notice. As soon as they were back in the bungalow, he picked up one of the motorbike magazines.

It was a while before the Major was able to get over to the Manor on his birthday plant quest. Other duties had called. Jumble sales, cake and coffee mornings, an unnerving lecture by a frightening woman entitled Training Your Dog and You, a very boring talk by someone else about The Jurassic World of Dorset which seemed to have happened a hell of a long time ago, not forgetting the annual endurance test of the village hall AGM.

Strenuous efforts had been required of him for all these events – unstacking and restacking the chairs, carrying stuff here, there and everywhere, hours spent hanging about waiting for things to start and, eventually, for them to stop. He had found himself with no time to call his own.

When Marjorie finally went off to one of her committee meetings, backing the protesting Escort out of the garage and narrowly missing the gatepost, he watched the car bounce away with relief. Peace at last! A quick snifter to set him up and he was off across the green towards the Manor.

He headed for the greenhouses where he remembered seeing plants for sale put outside on long benches. There were no other customers around and no sign of Tanya or anyone else. He took his time, wandering up and down the benches, pretending to examine the plants closely and hoping she would come by. No such luck. In the end, he picked up a tall plant with purple flowers and a long Latin name, which would impress the old girl. It gave him the excuse to wander about some more, searching for someone to pay. He caught sight of a woman in the distance, but the old peepers weren't quite up to scratch these days and before he could get closer, she'd vanished. Just as well. It might have been the golf widow – the last person he wanted to run into. He walked on and, as he was passing one of the greenhouses, the loony chap, Jacob, came blundering out straight into him, knocking Marjorie's Latin plant out of his hands. The Major then watched him rush off without a word of apology. Damned fool! What on earth was all the panic about?

He peered into the greenhouse. All quiet on the Western Front. Nothing to frighten the horses. Just green things growing up long strings towards the roof. There was a nice smell in the air and he suddenly realized that the green things were tomato plants. He could see big bunches of them hanging down, ripening away. He sniffed appreciatively, thinking that tomatoes smelled a whole lot better than they tasted. Chopped up in one of the old girl's salads they were all water and pips, but these seemed quite different.

He walked on, wondering if he dared risk picking one to test. Nobody around. Better make sure, though. It wouldn't do to get caught red-handed, as it were. He wrinkled his nose as he approached the far end of the greenhouse. There was a different smell now, not nearly as pleasant as the tomatoes. Not nice at all.

The Major stopped in his tracks.

Some chap was sprawled face down on the ground ahead, a wooden stool overturned beside him. He edged closer. Great Scot! Blood everywhere! He'd never seen so much of it in his life. All over the back of the man's head. Pools of it in the soil. A blood-soaked spade lying on the ground.

The Major clutched at his chest. He could feel the old ticker banging away like a hammer. Keep calm! Steady the Buffs! Rally the troops! He turned and bolted for the door.

NINE

The Colonel answered the phone, bracing himself for yet another round with his daughter-in-law on the subject of bungalows and vitamins. Instead, he heard Ruth's frantic voice.

'Hugh? Can you come at once? Something simply terrible has happened.'

He didn't waste time asking what it was. He sprinted for the Riley like one of The Few scrambling in 1940. As he skidded into the Manor driveway he saw several cars parked there – two of them marked police cars. Ruth opened the front door at once.

'Thank God you're here, Hugh!'

He made her sit down on one of the hall chairs. 'Tell me what's happened.'

'Lawrence Deacon has been murdered.'

'Murdered? Are you sure?'

'Unless he managed to commit suicide by hitting himself over the head with a spade, then, yes, I'm very sure. And so are the police. Inspector Squibb is here with them. You remember him?'

Indeed he did, and the memory was not at all agreeable. Inspector Squibb had been in charge of the investigation into Lady Swynford's death at the Manor. Ruth's mother had been suffocated with a pillow in her bedroom while the annual summer fête took place merrily in the gardens below. There had been a number of police suspects – one of them Ruth herself, who had happened to discover her mother's body – and the young Inspector Squibb, cocky and confident, had managed to make himself offensive to everyone. The Colonel had encountered him again when the famous actress, Lois Delaney, had been found dead in her bath at one of the Hall's newly converted flats and Squibb had reappeared to direct the proceedings. The second experience had been no improvement on the first.

'Where are the police?'

'Out in the greenhouse where Lawrence was found.'

'What was he doing there?'

'I'd asked him to pinch out the tomato side shoots for me. I showed him how to do it and gave him a stool so he could sit down whenever he wanted. Then I left him alone.'

'Who found his body?'

'The Major.'

'The Major?'

'Apparently, he'd come to choose a plant for Marjorie's birthday. He says he was looking for someone to pay when Jacob came rushing out of the greenhouse in a big panic, collided with him and ran off. When he went to look inside, wondering what was wrong, he saw someone lying on the ground, face down, with blood all over the place. Tanya heard the Major yelling for help and ran to the greenhouse. As soon as she saw Lawrence she came and fetched me from the stables.'

'She knew it was him? Even though he was lying face down?'

'She must have done. She told me it was him. I phoned Tom and he came home at once. He said Lawrence was dead and nothing could be done for him. He called the police and stayed till they arrived. Then he had to go and take evening surgery and I called you.'

'I'm very glad you did. Where's the Major now?'

'In the drawing room. On his third whisky. Inspector Squibb ordered him to wait there for further questioning. Poor old Major, he's pretty shaken up. Apparently, there was some blood on his blazer and Squibb's treating him like a major suspect. The Major, for heaven's sake! It's ridiculous.' She looked up at the Colonel. 'Do you think Jacob could have done it, Hugh? He's never hurt a fly, as far as I know, but he was very upset about having other people working in the gardens, and he didn't like Lawrence Deacon at all.'

'Have the police interviewed him?'

'They can't find him. He's vanished. Run off and hidden himself somewhere, I suppose. Just about the worst thing he could have done, isn't it?'

The worst thing Jacob could have done, the Colonel thought, would have been to murder Deacon. And it certainly seemed possible. Who could know what had been building up in his mind? What fears and uncertainties for his future?

'Where was Jacob working?'

'He'd been digging over the potato bed in the kitchen garden.'

'With a spade?'

'Yes, he would have used a spade.'

'The same one that was lying by Lawrence Deacon?'

'I don't know. There are several others, though Jacob often uses that particular one. It's very well made.'

'Was there any reason for him to go into the greenhouse?'

'The only one I can think of is that he probably didn't trust Lawrence to pinch out the tomatoes properly. I usually give the job to Jacob because he's very good at it – surprisingly nimble and quick with his fingers – whereas Lawrence was slow and clumsy. I only asked Lawrence to do it because he was getting very bored and needed something to keep him occupied. Oh, Hugh, it looks very bad for Jacob, doesn't it?'

He said, 'There's no proof of anything at the moment. Shall I have a word with the Major? See if I can calm things down there?'

'Would you, Hugh? Tanya's been looking after Alan but I ought to go and take him off her hands.'

A shirt-sleeved Major was slumped in an armchair in the Manor drawing room, glass cradled to his chest.

'What the devil are you doing here, Colonel?'

'Ruth called me. She's told me about Deacon.'

The Major gulped at the glass. 'Hardly knew the fellow. Only met him once to talk to, and it was only a few words. Inspector Squibb seems to think I might have had something to do with it. Me? I told him I was looking for a plant for my wife, minding my own business, and that lunatic comes tearing out of the greenhouse, knocks the plant out of my hands and runs off without a word. Plant a complete goner, I might say, after all the trouble I'd taken to choose the damned thing. Then I go in and find a dead body. Some chap lying on the ground, blood everywhere. I hadn't a clue who it was. Not till later.'

'It must have been quite a shock for you.'

The Major took another gulp from the glass. 'Bit of an understatement. Thought I was going to have a heart attack. And now the cops have taken my best blazer. They found blood on it, they say, so they're keeping it as evidence. Evidence of what? I'd like to know. I had nothing to do with any of it. That mad man must have had blood on his hands when he ran into me, after he'd bashed Deacon with a spade.' Yet another gulp at the glass. 'I've a good mind to take myself off. If the Inspector wants to talk to me again, he can come to Shangri-La.'

The Colonel said soothingly, 'I'd wait here, if I were you. It's always wise to cooperate with the police as much as possible.'

'Huh! You may be right, but it's still a damned disgrace to treat honest, law-abiding citizens like this. I can't imagine what Marjorie will say.'

The Colonel could imagine quite well. He fetched the whisky decanter and refreshed the Major's glass.

'Would you like me to give her a call? Tell her what's happened?'

'No point. She'll still be at her damned committee meeting. They go on for ever.'

'I'll wait with you, if you like.'

The Major said gruffly, 'Very good of you. Much obliged. I must say the whole thing's got me a bit rattled.'

'Understandably.'

'I mean, when Ursula Swynford got herself suffocated at least it was done decently with a pillow and no mess. Not like this time. The place looked like a slaughterhouse.'

Nearly an hour passed before Inspector Squibb came into the room. He was even sleeker and cockier than the Colonel remembered. Sharp suit, silk tie, hair artfully combed forward to disguise its retreat, and a time-added layer of confidence – or arrogance, depending how you interpreted it. His Sergeant Biddlecombe – a contrast with his baggy clothing and ruddy, country face – trundled along in his wake.

The Inspector said in his no-particular accent from no-particular place, 'No need for me to detain you, Colonel.'

'Major Cuthbertson has asked me to stay and I'm happy to do so.'

'I'm not quite so happy. I need to ask the Major some more questions concerning the murder of Lawrence Deacon. As far as I am aware, Colonel, you are not involved in any way.'

With Dutch courage to hand, the Major spoke up from the depths of his armchair.

'I'd like the Colonel to stay.'

A shrug. 'If you insist, Major.'

'I damn well do.'

'Very well.'

The Inspector sat down on a sofa, the Sergeant at the opposite end with his notebook at the ready. The Colonel remained standing by a window.

'Let's run through your account again, shall we, Major?'

'There's nothing more I can tell you, Inspector.'

'There's always more, sir. What time exactly did you arrive at the Manor?'

The Major didn't know. Some time after two, he thought. He hadn't looked at his watch, for God's sake. There'd been no reason to do so. Prompted relentlessly by the Inspector, he went through his story again.

'When you were looking for a plant for your wife, was anybody else in the vicinity?'

'Not a soul.'

'No other customers?'

'I didn't notice any.'

'None of the other workers?'

The Major frowned. 'I saw some woman in the distance but I don't know who it was – she was too far away. Then she disappeared.'

'How do you know it was a woman?'

'Because it looked like one.'

'What was she wearing?'

'No idea.'

'Was she old or young?'

'Don't know.'

'What sort of build?'

'Build?'

'Was she fat or thin? Heavy or light?'

The Major shrugged. 'She was only there for a few seconds and I couldn't see her properly. My sight's not so good these days.'

'But you're sure it was a woman?'

'I can tell the difference, Inspector.'

'What happened then?'

'That gardener chap, Jacob, came tearing out of the greenhouse and ran slap into me.'

'Did he say anything to you, sir?'

'Not a word. Not even sorry.'

'Did you say anything to him?'

'I think I said something like, "Mind where you're going". I might have put it a bit more strongly. He'd knocked the plant out of my hands and wrecked it.'

'What happened then?'

'I've already told you.'

'Tell me again.'

'I wondered what the hell had upset him so much and I went into the greenhouse to take a look. I couldn't see anything at first, then I saw a man lying on the ground at the far end. There was a stool knocked over beside him and I thought maybe he'd fallen off it and hurt himself.'

'You didn't recognize him?'

'How could I? He was face down and covered in blood.' The Major shuddered. 'There was a spade with blood all over it as well.'

'Did you touch or move anything?'

'Certainly not.'

'You're sure about that?'

'Of course I am.'

'But there was blood on your jacket.'

'I didn't touch a damn thing, Inspector. That maniac, Jacob, touched me when he ran into me.'

'Did you see blood on his hands?'

'No, but there must have been. It's obvious he killed Deacon.'

'So, what did you do next, Major, after you had discovered the body?'

'Just what I told you before. I ran out of the greenhouse and shouted for help. And Mrs Carberry came.'

'How long did she take to arrive?'

'A few minutes, I suppose.'

'And then?'

'I told her there was a body in the greenhouse. She took a look and then she went to find Mrs Harvey and tell her what had happened.'

'What did you do?'

'Waited outside the door.'

'You didn't go back inside?'

The Major shuddered again. 'No, I did not.'

'How did Mrs Harvey react to the news?'

'She was damned upset, of course. What do you think, Inspector? Ghastly thing to have someone murdered in your own home. Not the first time it's happened to her either.'

'Indeed it isn't. Most unfortunate. What did Mrs Harvey do?'

'She went to phone her husband and he turned up almost at once. He called the police as soon as he'd seen Deacon's body and been sure he was dead.'

The Inspector smoothed his tie carefully. 'What did you think of Mr Deacon, Major?'

'I didn't think of him at all. I'd only ever spoken to him once.'

'Well, what did people in Frog End think of him?'

'No idea.'

'People always talk about other people in villages, Major. You must have heard something. In the Dog and Duck, for example.'

'I don't listen to gossip, Inspector. Not my sort of thing. All I know is the chap had had a stroke a while ago and that Dr Harvey thought it'd do him good to get out and do a spot of gardening at the Manor.'

'Do you know Mr Deacon's wife?'

'Never even spoken to her. Only seen her once at the village hall. I think she runs some sort of shop in Dorchester. They were newcomers to Frog End, you know.'

'I'm aware of that.' The Inspector turned his head towards the window. 'Since you're staying, Colonel, it would be interesting to learn what you know about the Deacons.'

'I've never met Mrs Deacon either and only spoken to her husband a few times when he was working here.'

'How did he get on with Jacob? Or rather, how did Jacob get on with him?'

'The same way that Jacob gets on with most people, Inspector. You know how he is.'

'Crackers like the biscuit box he was dumped in as a baby. Yes, I know all about him, Colonel. And now he's absconded from the scene of a crime.'

'That's no proof that he committed it. He may have discovered Deacon's body and run away because he thought he'd be blamed. There's no record of violence attached to him, as you must know from your investigation into Lady Swynford's death when he was already working here.'

'But the man's hardly normal, is he, sir? And who knows how he might react if he felt his job and his cosy home at the Manor were being threatened.'

The Colonel hesitated. This was a murder investigation, which obliged him to help Inspector Squibb with his legitimate enquiries in any way that he could.

'Mrs Harvey thought that Jacob seemed rather unsettled by some of Dr Harvey's patients working here as a form of therapy. Dr Harvey had recommended it for Lawrence Deacon after his stroke. Mrs Carberry, Johnny Turner and Mrs Reed are also patients of his.'

'So Mrs Harvey told me. I've already spoken with Mrs Carberry who seems unlikely to have presented much of a worry to Jacob and I'm keeping an open mind about the wheelchair boy. I haven't questioned Mrs Reed yet but apparently she wasn't working at the Manor today. Mr Deacon could have been a different matter. What was he like as a person?'

The Colonel hesitated again. 'I think his stroke had affected him emotionally as well as physically. He seemed bitter about life.'

'Not what you would call an easy man?'

'Not a very happy one. Apparently, he and his wife lost their only son in a tragic accident many years ago and I don't think he ever got over the loss. But I don't see how his state of mind could have induced someone to murder him.'

'Bitter and unhappy people can cause a lot of trouble, Colonel. Whoever hit Mr Deacon's head with a spade must have had a strong reason for it, wouldn't you say? They did it several times, you know – to make very certain that he was dead.'

The Major spoke up again from his chair. 'How much longer are you going to keep me here, Inspector? It's damned inconvenient.'

'Oh, you can go now, Major. No more questions – for the time being.'

'Huh!' The Major put down his empty glass and stood up, squaring his shoulders. 'You coming, Colonel?'

He shook his head. 'Not yet. I'll see if Ruth needs any help.'

'Well, if you don't mind, I'll cut along. If Marjorie's home before me she'll be wondering where I am and there'll be hell to pay if I'm late for supper.'

'Don't be ridiculous, Roger! You've never killed anyone in your life – not even in the army when you were supposed to.'

It occurred to the Major that this was not necessarily a compliment from his wife.

'Well, Inspector Squibb seemed to think I must have had something to do with Deacon's murder. He asked me all sorts of questions. And the police have kept my blazer as evidence because that chap left blood on it. Damned nerve!'

'Squibb? I remember that young man from the time when he was investigating Ursula Swynford's death. A bully. He was just trying to frighten you, Roger. No one could believe you were capable of murder. Not in a hundred years.'

He should have been pleased and flattered by the old girl's faith and trust, but he wasn't.

'Well, somebody was. Definitely that loony, I'd say, judging by the way he was behaving. Several bricks short of a load, I've always reckoned, and now he's done a bunk.'

'He's harmless enough, or Ruth would never have kept him.'

'Then if he didn't do it, who did?'

'A stranger on the lookout for something to steal and Mr Deacon tried to stop him.'

The Major's voice rose several notches. 'I ask you, Marjorie, is that likely? Some passer by smashed Deacon's head in for a few tomatoes?'

'Now, calm down, Roger. Calm down.'

She was patting his hand. Not something he could remember her ever doing before. She probably thought he was losing his grip. Well, maybe he was. The whole thing had brought back the nightmare of Ursula Swynford getting bumped off during a Manor fête a couple of years ago. His blood still ran cold to think about it. He'd been manning the Bottle Stall tombola and he'd called out to Ursula as she'd swanned past doing her lady-of-the-manor act. Bit cheeky on his part, of course, but he'd thought everything was steaming along nicely between them. What with the racket from the band, he hadn't really heard what she'd answered and later on he'd sneaked up to her room, just to have a little chat about things. He'd found her lying dead as a dodo on the bed and scarpered p.d.q., thinking she'd had another stroke. As it had turned out, she'd been murdered. Murdered, for God's sake! He'd never told a soul about going to her room. Well, who would have believed he was innocent? Nobody but Marjorie, it seemed, which wasn't much comfort.

The old girl gave his hand another pat – more of a slap really.

'Inspector Squibb will deal with everything. I'd have another drink, if I were you. Supper in fifteen minutes.'

She got up to leave. As he'd expected, there was a parting shot from the doorway.

'Let that be a lesson to you, Roger.'

'A lesson?'

'To stay out of trouble in future.'

She was gone before he could think of a good riposte.

It was an effort to walk over to the cocktail cabinet. Still a bit wobbly on the pins. No need to rush it, though. He'd been given orders from the bridge, no less. Carte blanche, as the Frogs said. He opened the cabinet lid casually and the tinkling notes of 'Drink to Me Only' started up on cue.

He took his time with glass and bottle, humming along and remembering some of the words of the song. *Or leave a kiss within the cup, and I'll not ask for wine.* By Jove, that was saying something! He remembered a bit more. *The thirst that from the soul doth rise doth ask a drink divine; but might I of Jove's nectar sup, I would not change for thine.* Quite a racy song for an oldie, when he thought about it. Of course, anything went these days – too far, in his opinion. There was another verse but he'd forgotten the words. He left the lid up and the tune played on. For once, the damned thing could go on as loud and as long as it pleased.

He made his way back to the armchair and sat down again, his glass well-primed and at the ready. His old and trusted ally would soon do the trick and put everything back into perspective. One sip and he could feel his cockles warming up.

Marjorie was quite right. There was nothing to worry about. The Inspector would be on the case and have everything sorted out in a jiffy. Didn't care for the chap, personally, or for his attitude, but he was only doing his job. That was the important thing to remember.

The loony had done the deed – there wasn't much doubt about it – and a horrible deed it was. All that blood everywhere. It reminded him of the Shakespeare play the old girl had once dragged him to see. Who would have thought the old man to have had so much blood in him? Macbeth's wife had been wandering around in a real state, trying to wash it off her hands. *Out, damned spot! Out, I say!* He felt rather the same about his best blazer which had had not one but several spots on it. He wasn't quite so sure he wanted it back now.

He switched his thoughts to the woman he'd seen in the distance. Definitely a woman, no question about it. He knew the difference all right. Had known it for years. But who? The old mince pies had let him down but there had been something vaguely familiar about her, if only he could remember what it was.

Not that it mattered much, so far as he could see. Whoever she'd been she'd had nothing to do with it. No woman could have swung a heavy spade with that amount of force. It had been a man. An angry man. A very angry man indeed. A lunatic.

TEN

'We'll be going over to the Manor again tomorrow, Johnny.'

She'd spoken quite firmly, for a change.

He turned a page of the motorbike magazine. The pile was back beside the wheelchair. There had been no more gardening books.

'I'm not going if the cops are still there.'

'Mrs Harvey's just phoned to say the police have finished their investigations for the time being and would you be able to come and give her a hand again, if you don't mind.'

'I do mind.'

'Mrs Harvey needs you, Johnny. You've been such a help to her.'

'I told you before, she's just sorry for me. And I'm not going there again.'

'Please, Johnny. For my sake. You were getting on so well.'

'Everything's changed now.'

'But Mr Deacon won't be there. It was a horrible thing to happen, but at least you don't have to worry about him any more.'

'Shut up, Mum! I don't want to talk about it.'

Inspector Squibb and a Sergeant had come to see Johnny and the interview had not gone well. Johnny had refused to answer their questions properly. He didn't know, he'd said, or he couldn't remember. He'd been hoeing in the rose garden like he'd been told to and hadn't seen a thing. He'd ended up by saying outright that he thought Mr Deacon had got what he deserved.

When Sheila had been showing the two policemen out of the house she'd tried to smooth things over.

'Things haven't been easy for Johnny, Inspector. Not since his accident.'

He'd said nastily, 'They're not easy for us either, Mrs Turner.

This is a murder case. A very serious matter. There'll be an inquest and your son will find he has to answer questions in court whether he wants to or not. The truth, the whole truth and nothing but the truth.'

'But Johnny had nothing to do with it. He can't walk.'

'He didn't need to. From what I've heard he can get himself around the Manor gardens, no trouble. He's rather good at managing his wheelchair, by all accounts. Very nifty. If Mr Deacon was sitting down on that stool in the greenhouse, back turned, all your son had to do was wheel himself up very quietly behind him and hit him over the head very hard with a spade. It took considerable strength to inflict those wounds, Mrs Turner. Johnny's legs may not work, but his arms certainly do. Better than most people's because they get lots of exercise. I'd say he could easily have done it.'

She'd found her voice. 'He hardly knew Mr Deacon.'

'Well, he doesn't seem to have liked him much, does he? Not from the way he spoke about him. There must have been a reason.'

'He's never said anything to me.'

'He wouldn't, would he? He doesn't say much to anyone, so I'm told. Keeps everything to himself, isn't that so? Quite the dark horse. Don't worry, Mrs Turner. We'll soon find out what it was.'

When they'd gone, she'd said to Johnny brightly, 'I'll make us a cup of tea, shall I?'

He gave one of his don't care shrugs and turned another page.

She put the kettle on, took down the teapot and set out two cups and saucers on the tray. Her hands were shaking so much that the china rattled.

'What on earth are we going to do, Tom?'

'Carry on, Ruth. As we always do.'

'I can't do that. I can't behave as though nothing has happened.' She was close to feeble tears. 'It's been another nightmare – the police swarming all over the Manor again, the Inspector insinuating things just like he did when my mother died. He seems to think Lawrence's murder was all our fault – that gardening therapy is some quack idea that was bound to end in trouble.'

'There's nothing quack about it.'

'But does it really work?'

'You've seen how well it was working with Johnny.'

'Not any more. He won't come near us. Nor will Mrs Reed. She says her husband has forbidden her to come to the Manor again. Tanya's the only one who's been turning up, but I'm not sure how long she'll last. She's very jumpy and not at all happy. We may not think Jacob's guilty, Tom, but I keep remembering how upset he was by the others coming to help here, and he's the only one who would have had the strength to use a spade like that. Joyce Reed can barely lift a pair of secateurs and Tanya has never done any sort of physical work before. That leaves Johnny in his wheelchair or the Major in his best blazer buying a plant for his wife. It must have been Jacob. There's nobody else.'

'He didn't do it, Ruth.'

'If he's innocent, why did he run off and hide?'

'He's been hiding for most of his life, one way or another. When he discovered the body he thought, quite rightly, that he'd be suspected. So, he fled.'

She said, 'I'm frightened, Tom. Supposing he comes back here? He might be blaming us. He might harm Alan.'

He put his arms round her. 'Jacob would never hurt anyone, I promise you. And the police will find him soon.'

'Bloody awful thing to have happened, Hugh. Poor Ruth! She must be very cut up. Another murder at the Manor. It's getting to sound like an Agatha Christie.'

The Colonel poured a slightly stiffer Chivas Regal than usual and handed the glass to Naomi.

'I know. It's very bad news.'

'You were over there this morning, so what's the latest?'

'Tom's seeing to his patients, Ruth's trying to carry on as normal with no Jacob and only Tanya left to help her. The police have gone over everything with a fine toothcomb and gone. For the moment.'

'Fingerprints?'

'Undoubtedly. They've done Jacob's room over as well as the greenhouse and they took the spade away with them.'

'Exhibit A?'

'Well, it's the murder weapon, there's no doubt about that.'

'And Jacob is Suspect Number One?'

'It would seem so. For the moment, at least. They still haven't found him and they're searching hard.'

'Poor chap. He must be holed up somewhere and absolutely terrified. But he's no murderer, Hugh. He couldn't say boo to a goose. We know that. You'll just have to solve the mystery and save his skin.'

'Me?'

'Well, you usually work out whodunnit, don't you? Put your mind to this one.'

'That's Inspector Squibb's job.'

'Oh, the man's useless. It's no good waiting around for him. Get your thinking cap on, Hugh. What about Deacon's wife as a suspect? Maybe she got fed up with him moaning about his health. Men can be soooo boring when they're ill – or think they are. Cecil used to drive me crazy. Always something wrong. I often used to feel like killing him.'

'As far as I'm aware, Mrs Deacon was working in her gift shop in Dorchester at the time her husband was murdered.'

'Does she have an alibi?'

'Presumably there were customers who could supply her with one. The police are bound to have checked. I don't believe she did it.'

There had been a service for Lawrence Deacon at the local crematorium and the Colonel had attended as a courtesy, together with a handful of mourners. Afterwards, he had introduced himself to Mrs Deacon who had impressed him. She had been very calm and composed. A young-looking, attractive woman and nothing whatsoever like a vengeful murderess.

Naomi was less convinced. 'She could have shut up shop between customers, nipped over to the Manor, given him a bash or two over the head with a spade and been back in the shop again in a jiffy.'

'Someone would have noticed her at the Manor, don't you think?'

'Not necessarily, Hugh. Customers always have all their attention on the plants while they're trying to decide which ones to buy. I've watched them dithering for hours, picking them up and putting them down, like people choosing pork chops in Waitrose. You could ride an elephant past and they wouldn't see it. I certainly wouldn't cross her off the list.'

Naomi peered into her glass as though in search of further inspiration.

'Now, let me think who else might have done it. I know, Tanya Carberry. Our grief-stricken widow. Perhaps Deacon tried it on with her? I always thought there was something a bit creepy about him, you know. Men go for widows, apparently. They think they're easy game. Though I can't say I've ever had to deal with that problem myself.'

'I'm sure you'd be very capable of handling it, Naomi.'

'You're right there. But someone like Tanya might not find it quite so easy. She was in a real state after her husband died, you know. Down at rock bottom. The gardening has done wonders to restore her, but maybe Deacon upset her with some unwelcome attentions. Tipped her back over the edge.'

'Unlikely.'

'Well, we can rule out Johnny as a suspect, can't we? He's non-combatant unless he miraculously recovered the use of his legs. And the Major too, of course, in spite of his blood-stained blazer. He'd never kill anyone with a garden spade – it wouldn't be cricket. And Joyce Reed wasn't at work that day, was she? So that lets her off the hook, too.'

'I don't think the Inspector is ruling anyone out at the moment.'

'I told you, Hugh, Squabb's hopeless.'

'Squibb.'

'Whatever he's called. You're going to have to take over. Do your stuff.'

Thursday had appeared from the direction of the pond where he had been admiring the goldfish. He steered a path round the side of the sundowner terrace keeping a careful distance from dog-person Naomi. He had never been a fat cat, in any sense, but the Colonel noticed that he was looking much thinner than usual. Worryingly so.

'Hugh? Are you listening to me?'

He said slowly, 'I'm listening, Naomi.'

'Well?'

'I'll do whatever I can.'

She waved her whisky glass at him.

'See that you do.'

'I was wondering if any progress had been made on the Deacon case, Inspector?'

Squibb, installed behind a big desk in his police station office, oozed self-importance.

'I'll let you know when the time is appropriate, Colonel.'

'As you can imagine, Mrs Harvey's very upset.'

'I would be too, if I was in her shoes. One murder at the Manor was bad enough but two is getting careless, don't you agree?'

'Mrs Harvey had no part in either.'

'Not in her mother's murder, I grant you, but Mr Deacon's assailant is unknown at the moment. Anyone present at the Manor on that day could have killed him and that includes Mrs Harvey. I'm proceeding on that basis.'

The Colonel said, 'I understood that Jacob was your prime suspect.'

'Did you, sir? Then you'd be wrong. I always keep an open mind.'

'But you're still looking for him?'

'That's right, sir. You know his background. I remember we discussed it in detail when Lady Swynford was murdered. Abandoned on a doorstep in a biscuit box, then several years in an orphanage, and more years in a mental hospital before he somehow managed to worm his way into working at the Manor. You told me yourself that Mrs Harvey said he seemed upset by Dr Harvey's patients starting to do garden work at the Manor. Frightened he'd lose his cushy billet, I'd say. And from what I've learned, Mr Deacon was the type who'd do a thorough job of worrying him. So, yes, we're still looking for

Jacob and we'll be asking him a lot of questions when we find him, which we will. Meantime, as I said, I'm proceeding with my investigations. And I'm afraid I can't give you any more of my time, sir.'

The Colonel ran into Mrs Reed after he had left the police station. She had been changing her library book, she told him, though it was a waste of time since they never had anything decent to read. Nothing but trashy novels or ghosted autobiographies by tenth-rate celebrities, in her opinion.

He said drily, 'I've been wasting my time too. Talking to Inspector Squibb.'

'He came to my flat at the Hall and asked me a whole lot of questions to do with Mr Deacon's murder. I told him that I wasn't at the Manor that day, or anywhere near it, so I couldn't help him. I must say it's all been very stressful and bad for my health. I've told Mrs Harvey that I can't do any more gardening work for her until the police have found Jacob and arrested him.'

'He may not be guilty.'

'The Major saw him running out of the greenhouse and there was blood all over his hands. He must be. My husband says it's not safe for me to go back.'

The Colonel said, 'As a matter of interest, what was your opinion of Lawrence Deacon?'

'The Inspector asked me that too.'

'What was your answer?'

'I thought he was a most unpleasant man. He treated Jacob disgracefully. I'm not surprised the worm turned.'

The Inspector had used the same word in connection with Jacob but there was really nothing worm-like about Jacob. Worms were actually bold creatures, advancing sinuously but inexorably through life whereas Jacob was a timid and terrified animal, unable to communicate, unable to cope, defenceless. Flight would always be his instinctive way out of trouble – unless he had been cornered and there was no escape.

The Colonel raised his cap. 'Well, I hope to see you back at the Manor very soon, Mrs Reed.'

'Most unlikely, I'm afraid.'

As he moved on, she called after him. 'Arthur's won another trophy.'

'My congratulations.'

She shrugged. 'It's just one more to polish.'

Why were they kept so brightly polished and so prominently on show, the Colonel wondered, unless she was, in fact, proud of her husband? The resentful golf widow could be a pretence, kept up over years. A game that suited both the Reeds, for some strange reason. You never knew the whole truth about other people's marriages or what went on behind closed doors. It was a secret and usually very well kept.

ELEVEN

On his next trip into Dorchester, the Colonel stopped at Mrs Deacon's shop. Naomi had given him the name and location. He must have passed it often but this time he took a look in the window. Gift shops weren't really for him, but he could see that Seek and Find was much better than most. The items for sale were well chosen, well displayed and well lit. He opened the door and an old-fashioned bell jangled as he went inside.

Claudia Deacon was busy serving a customer and he waited until she had finished. Once again, he was impressed by her efficient look and by her calm demeanour. Outwardly, at least, she seemed unaffected by the loss of her husband, but he had long ago learned that some people chose to hide their feelings, to keep them private. Their previous meeting after the funeral service had been very brief, but she remembered him.

'How nice to see you again, Colonel. Are you looking for something to buy, or is this a different sort of visit?'

He said frankly, 'A different sort. I was wondering how you were coping with Inspector Squibb and his cohorts?'

'He's a fairly objectionable man, isn't he? I'm quite sure I'm high on his list of suspects but he's finding it rather hard to unearth any evidence that I murdered my husband.'

'I wouldn't take it personally. He always suspects everyone.'

'You've come across him before, then?'

'Unfortunately.'

'In Frog End?'

'Yes, indeed.'

'Another murder?'

'Two, actually, though one was never proved.'

'I'm very surprised. It seems such a quiet place.'

'Appearances are often deceptive.'

'That's true.' She looked him straight in the eye. 'It wasn't me who murdered Lawrence. I was working here in the shop all that day, as I told the Inspector, and there were plenty of customers in here to confirm it.'

'I don't doubt you, Mrs Deacon.'

'I won't deny that our relationship had been deteriorating for a number of years and that Lawrence's stroke had made it even worse. He found the effects very hard to cope with. So did I, to be honest. It was a difficult situation for us both – him stuck alone at home, me working here all hours. He resented it. I have a girl who comes in to give me a hand part-time but otherwise I do everything myself. The shop means a great deal to me. It's become very important in my life.'

'And I can see that you've made a great success of it.'

'Unfortunately, Lawrence didn't like the idea at all. He thought he should come first and that I should give up the shop and stay at home to hold his hand. I refused and kept on refusing. When Dr Harvey suggested the gardening therapy to him I was all in favour because I thought it might really do him some good. But Lawrence wasn't so keen. He never took to it, you know. It bored him and so it never worked. And lately, for some reason, he'd got the idea into his head that I was having an affair.' She smiled. 'I might have been tempted, but I don't have the time, or the energy.'

'He told me that you and he lost your only son some years ago.'

'I'm surprised that he said anything about it, but then I can see that you're the kind of person people would confide in. We never spoke of Richard. We agreed not to after he died. I think some people find it a comfort to talk about a lost loved one but we both found it agonising.'

'I'm sorry to have mentioned it.'

'You're not the first, Colonel. The Inspector has already brought up the subject, though it has nothing whatever to do with Lawrence's murder. How could it? Richard was killed more than twenty years ago when he was seventeen. He was the pillion passenger on a motorbike. His best friend had just bought one and they went out for a spin – at top speed, of course, like all boys. They went round a corner too fast and into a skid. The friend stayed on the bike and survived, but Richard was thrown off and hit a tree. He died instantly.'

'I'm so sorry.'

'It might have been more bearable if we'd had other children, but we didn't. As it was, the only way we could cope with the loss was to bury it deep and not to speak of him any more. He was a lovely boy, you see. Very special. Charming, kind, good-natured, funny, so full of life . . . It broke us both completely. Our marriage was never the same again.'

The Colonel said, 'Another of Dr Harvey's patients working at the Manor is a young man called Johnny Turner. He's confined to a wheelchair after a motorbike accident which damaged his spine irreparably. Did Lawrence ever talk about him to you?'

'Oh, yes. Several times. He wasn't at all sympathetic, I'm afraid. He said it served him right. He never forgave Richard's friend, you see. The friend survived the accident that he'd caused, and without a scratch, while Richard was killed. It didn't seem fair to Lawrence. But, of course, that sort of thing happens all the time, especially to reckless young men. After all, they are the ones who have to fight our wars for us, aren't they, Colonel? They have the nerve and courage it takes. They don't believe in death happening to them. It's something that happens to someone else.' She paused. 'I'm sure Lawrence felt that your young Johnny in his wheelchair represented some sort of retribution. He, at least, hadn't got away with it scot-free, like Richard's friend and, better still, he would be paying the price slowly for the rest of his life. The idea would have given Lawrence a great deal of satisfaction, and I've no doubt he talked about it to other people. That's the sort of person he'd become, especially since his stroke. Bitter and twisted. I'm not really surprised that somebody killed him.'

She had spoken matter-of-factly, without emotion.

'Do you have any idea who it might have been?'

'I'm afraid not. But, as I told you, it wasn't me.'

The Colonel said, 'I expect you know that Jacob, the gardener who works for Mrs Harvey, was seen running away from the greenhouse just before your husband's body was discovered.'

'Inspector Squibb told me. I gather Major Cuthbertson definitely identified him. I've only been to the Manor once and I've never actually met Jacob. He's gone missing, hasn't he? Which must put him ahead of me on the Inspector's list.'

'What did your husband think of Jacob?'

'Bats in the belfry was one term he used. Or crackers like the Jacobs Cream Cracker box he was found in as a baby. That's why he was named Jacob, apparently. Lawrence thought that was very funny. He made jokes about it.'

'To Jacob?'

'To me and probably to others. I don't know about to Jacob. I imagine Jacob kept well away from Lawrence. I expect he was frightened of him. He could be very unpleasant and cruel. Tell me, Colonel, why are you so interested in my husband's murder? You can't have known him very well. Why should you care who killed him, or why?'

'Frog End would like to see the mystery solved, Mrs Deacon.'

'You mean the whole village?'

'More or less.'

'And you think you can solve it?'

'I can only try.'

'Well, I wish you luck. The police don't seem to be getting anywhere, do they?'

'Not so far.'

She said, 'Lawrence wanted me to go away with him to Paris, you know. We went there once years ago, soon after we were married, and he wanted us to go back and stay in a smart hotel. I suppose he thought we could somehow go back to being the young couple we once were.'

'What did you say?'

'I said I couldn't leave the shop at the busiest time of the year. He was furious, of course. He said it was just an excuse and that I didn't want to go with him, which was perfectly true, I didn't. I'm afraid I told him so straight out. I wouldn't go so far as to say I hated him, Colonel, but I didn't like what he had become. Of course, that didn't help our situation, but it had nothing to do with his murder.'

'Could it have caused him to lash out at somebody else, do you think? To vent his feelings?'

'I suppose so. He certainly never held back from speaking his mind. He didn't care about people any more.'

Another customer came in and the Colonel took his leave.

He called at the pet shop to buy Thursday some tins of the kind of food that might particularly tempt him – the ones with fancy names: Grilled Fish Medley, Tempting Terrine of Salmon, Duck Delight. Lately, the old cat had been even more picky than usual.

As he drove back home in the Riley, he thought about his talk with Claudia Deacon. He had appreciated her honesty. She had freely admitted that her relationship with her husband had been far from perfect, but that was no motive for murder. She could have left him at any time. By her own admission, Claudia Deacon hadn't liked what her husband had become, but whoever had smashed the spade down on Deacon's skull had done so with far deeper and stronger feelings than dislike. Rage? Fear? Hatred? Revenge? Claudia could have felt any, or all, of these but kept them well hidden.

Meanwhile, the inquest on Lawrence Deacon's death had been adjourned, pending further police investigations.

And Jacob was still missing.

Instead of driving back to his cottage, the Colonel turned into The Close leading to the new bungalows. He went past Journey's End, The Nook, Tree Tops and Shangri-La before he reached the one with the beautiful pelargonium in a blue pot standing by the front door. Ruth had told him the story. Johnny had apparently bought the plant out of his wages. Ruth had watched him choosing it very carefully – Lara Starshine with the bright pink flowers. She had seen how moved Mrs Turner had been when Johnny had given it to her: the first sign of any appreciation or gratitude from her son. It must have been quite a moment.

The Colonel parked the Riley and walked up to the door. It was some time before it was opened to him and not by Mrs Turner, as he had expected, but by Johnny.

'Mum's not here. She's gone on the bus to Dorchester.'

He had stopped to speak to Mrs Turner on several occasions when they had passed each other as she was pushing the wheelchair round the green and he had always included Johnny in the conversation, though with very limited success. The boy, hunched up in his chair, seldom responded.

'Would you mind if I came in for a moment, Johnny?'

A shrug.

'Please yourself.'

The Colonel followed the wheelchair down the narrow hallway and into a sitting room. He could see how hard Mrs Turner had tried to make it cheerful with patterned curtains, bright cushions and pictures on the walls. There was a pile of magazines in a corner – some of them strewn untidily across the floor. Motorbike magazines. Nothing about gardening.

Johnny had spun the wheelchair on its axis to face him. He manoeuvred it like a dodgem car.

'The police have already been here, asking me questions. I've got nothing more to say about Mr Deacon, except what I told them. He got what he deserved.'

'I'm not the police, Johnny.'

'Why are you here, then?'

'I came to ask if you'd carry on at the Manor – like you did before. There's only Mrs Carberry left to help Mrs Harvey now.'

'She can get someone else – a proper gardener.'

'You were well on the way to becoming one.'

'No, I wasn't. It was all a con to make me feel like I was a normal person. Well, it didn't work. I'm not normal. I'm a bloody cripple and it's all I'll ever be.'

'That's up to you, Johnny.'

'What's that supposed to mean?'

'Well, you can choose to do nothing – just sit around here and read these magazines – or you can go out and do something else. It doesn't have to be gardening at the Manor but you happen to be rather good at that and Mrs Harvey happens to need you, so it makes some sense.'

'I'm not going there any more – not with the police hanging round, acting like I might have killed the bloke.'

'But you didn't kill him, did you?'

'I'm not saying I did or I didn't. I'm not saying anything.'

'Do you know who did?'

'I told you, I'm not saying.'

'Do you think it was Jacob?'

Another shrug.

'Dr and Mrs Harvey have done their best for you, Johnny, and now they need any help you can give them in return. Is there anything you saw or heard or know that might lead to the truth about Mr Deacon's murder? Anything at all?'

Silence.

The Colonel picked up one of the magazines from the floor. He turned the pages.

'You can do better than this, Johnny. Much better.'

'And you can go to hell.'

He left. He didn't blame Johnny in the least for how he felt. What right had he to lecture him? None whatsoever. It was Johnny's life to live exactly however he chose.

'I'd like another word with you, Mrs Carberry. If you don't mind.'

It was obvious that whether she minded or not, the Inspector was going to come into the flat. Tanya stood back and he walked past her, the Sergeant plodding after him.

'What exactly did you want to see me about, Inspector?'

'Perhaps we could sit down?'

'I've nothing to add to what I told you.'

'I'm sure we'll find that you have, Mrs Carberry.' He sat down, uninvited; so did the Sergeant who opened his notebook on his knee. 'Let's start by you telling me your movements on the day that Mr Deacon was murdered. From the time when you arrived at the Manor.'

She sat down as far away from him as possible. 'I've already done so.'

'Tell me again.'

She took a deep breath. The man was trying to unnerve her but if she kept her head, he couldn't actually do anything. He couldn't arrest her – not without proper evidence. The law was on her side.

'I was later than usual. I didn't get there until after ten o'clock.'

'Mrs Harvey didn't mind?'

'Mrs Harvey lets me come and go whenever I like.'

'That must be very convenient for you. I wish I had a job like that.'

'It's not a job, Inspector. I'm not a paid employee. I'm a patient of Dr Harvey's. The four of us were his patients. Mr Deacon, Mrs Carberry, Johnny and myself. Dr Harvey believes that gardening can be therapeutic in some circumstances.'

'I'm wondering what the circumstances were in your case, Mrs Carberry. Do you mind telling me the nature of your illness?'

Again, she minded very much but a refusal would be unwise.

'My husband died suddenly a year ago. I've been very depressed since.'

'And Dr Harvey has been treating you for that?'

'Yes.'

'But you don't need to work? To have a proper job?'

'No.'

'Your husband left you well-provided for?'

It was absolutely none of his business.

'I don't have any money worries, Inspector, if that's what you mean.'

'How about children?'

'I have two. Both grown-up and independent. My son lives in San Diego. My daughter in Seattle.'

'So, you don't see much of them?'

'Not a great deal.'

Hardly ever, she might have said, more truthfully.

'Are they married?'

'No, neither of them. Inspector, what exactly has all this got to do with Mr Deacon's murder?'

'I ask the questions, Mrs Carberry. Not you. How long have you lived in Frog End?'

'I've already told you that.'

'Tell me again.'

'We moved here just over a year ago. My husband died suddenly a few months later.'

'Leaving you all alone in a strange village?'

'The people here have been very kind.'

'But you must miss your husband?'

'Of course.'

'What sort of relationship did you have with the other patients?'

'I didn't have a lot to do with them. I was usually working on my own.'

'Going back to the day of Mr Deacon's murder, what garden work did you do – when you finally arrived at the Manor after ten?'

She repeated her story. Mrs Harvey had asked her to do some weeding in the herbaceous borders by the main lawn and she had spent the morning there. Around midday she had taken her sandwiches to eat in the old stables where there was a table and chairs. Mrs Harvey was often there too but not on that day.

'What about Mr Deacon?'

'He always ate his lunch wherever he was working. Johnny Turner sometimes joined me in the stables but not then.'

'Where was he?'

'I think he was hoeing in the rose garden. He must have had his sandwiches there.'

'So you didn't see Johnny at all?'

'Not until later.'

'Later?'

'He came to the greenhouse after Mr Deacon's body had been discovered. I expect he'd heard all the noise.'

'Noise?'

'Major Cuthbertson shouting for help.'

'Which direction did Johnny come from?'

'I didn't notice. The rose garden, I suppose.'

'What do you think of Johnny?'

'I'm very sorry for him. Anyone would be.'

'But not Mr Deacon, apparently. I gather he was fond of telling people that Johnny deserved everything that had happened to him.'

'I never heard him say that.'

'Do you think he ever said it to Johnny?'

'Not as far as I know.'

There was a pause while the Sergeant flicked over a page of his notebook. The Inspector went on. 'What about Jacob?'

'What about him?'

'Did you see him at any time during the afternoon?'

'No, I didn't see him at all.'

'Did you see Mr Deacon that morning?'

'He came past the border where I was weeding.'

'And stopped to talk to you?'

'Only for a moment.'

'What about?'

You don't have to tell him, she reminded herself. He can't know. Nobody can.

'He told me he'd been pinching out tomato side shoots and what a boring job it was. He was taking a break.'

'Did you like Mr Deacon?'

'I hardly knew him.'

'But what was your general impression of him?'

'He didn't seem a very cheerful sort of person. Of course, he was still recovering from a stroke.'

'Did he ever make any kind of unwelcome advances to you?'

She said coldly, 'I don't encourage that sort of thing, Inspector. I'm not interested. My late husband and I were very close.'

He changed tack. 'Where were you when you heard Major Cuthbertson shouting out for help?'

'I was back weeding the border.'

'Had you gone straight there from the stables after your lunch?'

'Yes.'

'What did you do when you heard the Major?'

'I ran to the greenhouse.'

'And then?'

'I've already told you.'

'Tell me again.'

She went on doggedly with the same account: the Major in a state of severe shock, the hideous scene in the greenhouse, the overturned stool, the body, the spade, the blood. And there were still more questions.

'When you first saw it, were you aware that the body was Mr Deacon's?'

'Yes, I was.'

'Even though he was lying face down and his head was covered in blood?'

'I recognized his clothes.'

'You were familiar with them? Yet you say you hardly knew him?'

'He always wore the same things for work.'

'What sort of things?'

'A grey woollen jumper, a check shirt and brown corduroy trousers.'

'Very observant of you, Mrs Carberry. Most people never notice details like that. So, after you had recognized Mr Deacon's clothes, what did you do then?'

'I went to find Mrs Harvey.'

'Where was she?'

'In the house.'

'What was she doing there?'

'Giving her baby, Alan, lunch.'

'You hadn't touched Mr Deacon, or attempted to move him?'

'Of course not.'

The Inspector smoothed his silk tie carefully, like stroking a cat.

'I understand that you're still working at the Manor, Mrs Carberry?'

'Yes, I am.'

'Doesn't it upset you?'

'I didn't want to let Mrs Harvey down, Inspector.'

'I don't suppose you're aware that this is the second murder to take place there in recent years.'

The second murder?

'No, I didn't know that.'

'Lady Swynford, Mrs Harvey's mother, was suffocated with a pillow in her bedroom during a summer fête.'

'How terrible! Did the police find out who did it?'

'Oh, yes. I was in charge of the investigation myself so you don't need to worry that the murderer is still at large. Tell me, Mrs Carberry, had you ever met either Mr Deacon or his wife before you came to live in Frog End?'

'No, never.'

'Are you sure about that?'

'Quite sure.'

There were more questions – some old, some new. As far as she could, she told the truth. He can't know, she kept telling herself. He can't possibly know.

Miss Butler knocked at the front door of Pond Cottage. A very timid knock, in case the Colonel was busy, or perhaps at work in his shed in the back garden. It wasn't quite clear what he did in there but she was aware that for some reason gentlemen liked to shut themselves away in sheds and not to be disturbed.

There was no question of her going round the side of the cottage. Mrs Cuthbertson, she understood, had been known to do so, and one or two other village ladies with similar nerve, but she had also heard that the Colonel never permitted any of them across the shed threshold. Not even Naomi Grimshaw, though she had often tried. The shed was apparently kept under lock and key and sacks hung across the inside of the windows. Of course, the Colonel was always most welcoming at Pond Cottage, but his shed was another story.

She knocked at the cottage door once more, prepared to leave, but this time the Colonel opened it, inviting her inside.

'Can I offer you a cup of tea, Miss Butler?'

'I wouldn't want to put you to any trouble, Colonel.'

'You won't. I've just put the kettle on. Shall we go into the sitting room? Milk but no sugar, isn't it?'

The cat, Thursday, was curled up in his winter place at the fire end of the sofa. Since it was now high summer and the grate empty, Miss Butler would have expected him to be out of doors, hunting things, but then he must be getting old, like everybody else. Rather to her relief, he took no notice as she sat down at the other end. She had nothing against cats, but it had to be said that the stray was no beauty – a battle-scarred thing with motley black and tan fur and a badly torn ear. The Colonel had been very good to give him a home. If he had turned up at Lupin Cottage, she, personally, would have shooed him away.

The Colonel brought her a cup of tea – a proper bone china

cup and saucer, not an ugly mug like most people seemed to use these days. He sat down in the wing-back tapestry chair opposite – a very fine and solid piece of antique furniture which she thought suited him well. After dark, with the lamps on and the curtains still open, she could see him sitting there from her front window.

'Is there anything I can do for you, Miss Butler?'

'Well, not exactly, Colonel . . . it's just something that I felt you should know.'

'Oh?'

'But perhaps you already do?'

He smiled at her.

'I'm afraid we won't know if I know until you tell me what it is.'

Such a gentleman, she thought. Others might well have been impatient at her inability to express herself clearly and succinctly, but not the Colonel. She plunged on.

'Well, you see, I just happened to be looking out of my sitting-room window when I noticed Inspector Squibb passing in his car.'

Fortunately, the binoculars had been close to hand and she had been able to monitor the car's progress round the green.

'Really?'

'I saw the car turn into the entrance to the Hall where Mr Deacon's widow lives. Mrs Carberry has a flat there too, of course, and Mr and Mrs Reed recently moved into Number 2 on the ground floor – as I'm sure you are aware, Colonel. I understand you've called.'

'Yes, indeed.'

'Rather an unlucky flat, I feel, don't you?'

'It certainly has an unfortunate history.'

'Quite. Naturally, they would all have been interviewed by the Inspector at the time of Mr Deacon's shocking murder. Mrs Reed wasn't actually working at the Manor on that day, as I understand it, but I'm sure the Inspector would have included her in his general enquiries, don't you think? Checked her story?'

'Almost certainly.'

'He's nothing if not thorough. So, it occurred to me that

the Inspector must be intending to question one of them again, if you see what I mean.'

'I think I do.'

Miss Butler paused, collecting her thoughts. It was important to get the facts right and in the right order.

'It was just before ten o'clock. I had seen Mrs Deacon leaving at a quarter past eight, as usual, to open her shop in Dorchester – she's always very punctual – and so I deduced that it was most likely Mrs Carberry whom the Inspector had gone to see, since Mrs Reed can't have had much to add to what she had already told him if she wasn't even there. If you follow me.'

'Yes, I follow you.'

'Anyway, Inspector Squibb was there for a long time. An hour and a half, in fact. I timed it by my watch, which is very reliable. I had it in the WRNS and it's never failed me. Which means that Mrs Carberry must be under suspicion. I thought you should know, Colonel – unless, of course, you knew already.'

'No, I didn't know, Miss Butler. But I think you may be jumping to conclusions. Inspector Squibb is making enquiries into a murder and he will need to gather as much information as he can from every source. It's normal police routine and it takes time.'

'Mrs Carberry is quite a stranger to the village, you see. An unknown quantity. And we never had a chance to get to know her husband before he died so suddenly.'

He said mildly, 'That doesn't make her a murderer.'

Her cheeks turned pink. 'No, of course not. But I just wondered if perhaps there had been something going on between Mrs Carberry and Mr Deacon.'

'I think that's very unlikely.'

'I agree that he didn't seem at all her type. So, if it wasn't Mrs Carberry who killed Mr Deacon it must have been someone else, mustn't it?'

'That's right. It must have been.'

She looked at him earnestly, clutching at the handbag on her lap.

'We're all depending on you, Colonel.'

'For what exactly, Miss Butler?'

'To find the murderer, of course.'

It had taken some time for Miss Butler to leave, during which the Colonel had done his best to convince her that he was not Sherlock Holmes, Lord Peter Wimsey and Hercule Poirot rolled into one, and that he had no more clues about the murderer's identity than anybody else. Miss Butler had remained stubbornly hopeful. She, Naomi and an untold number of others in Frog End were apparently expecting him to conjure up a satisfactory solution out of thin air. And do it fast.

The phone rang and it was Ruth.

'Squibb has just paid us another visit, Hugh.'

'Any news?'

'He says Jacob's fingerprints are on the spade handle. Not exactly conclusive evidence, of course . . . Jacob's used that spade hundreds of times before.'

'Where was it kept?'

'In the tool shed, along with all the other tools. Sometimes they get left lying about but mostly they're cleaned up and put away at the end of the day. Jacob has always been very good about doing that.'

'Were there any other prints on the spade?'

'Not according to the Inspector. Only Jacob's. They searched his room yet again and took away an old scarf. Squibb says they're going to use tracker dogs to hunt for him. Poor Jacob! Hunted down like an animal.'

'Do you have any idea where he might be hiding?'

'None at all. As far as we know, he has no friends. He never goes anywhere and he seems to have had a miserably lonely life. He's very odd, of course – as we all know – but Tom absolutely doesn't believe he'd attack someone, let alone kill them savagely. He thinks he'd run a mile sooner than do anything like that.'

The Colonel hoped Jacob had run many miles, for his own sake.

'Did Inspector Squibb have anything else to say?'

'Only that they'd found out that the blood on the Major's

blazer definitely belonged to Lawrence Deacon. So, I'm afraid he won't be getting it back for a while – if ever.'

The Major was at his post at the Dog and Duck, putting the world to rights.

'Too many damned foreigners let into this country, if you ask me. All kinds of odds and sods up to no good and jabbering away in some lingo nobody understands a word of. The Yanks can come if they want – they don't count as foreign and they get by in English – but the rest of the buggers ought to be kept out. Drawbridge up for the lot of 'em.'

The Colonel approached the bar. 'The other half, Major?'

'I don't mind if I do.'

'I hear the police are holding on to your blazer.'

'Huh! Damned nerve! They still can't find that lunatic, you know. Hounds baying all over the countryside and not a sniff of him. The Inspector had the gall to come round and ask me a whole lot more questions, even though it's an open and shut case. They've got fingerprints and blood. What more does he want?'

'Proof?'

'My God, I practically saw the chap do the deed in front of my eyes. I'm their star witness, though you'd never think so. They've been bothering Mrs Turner too. Damned bad show! I saw Squibb knocking at her door – as if the poor woman hasn't got enough to worry about, coping with that son of hers. I watch her pushing him backwards and forwards past us in that wheelchair and I don't know how she does it. Nothing to her but skin and bone. I hope she told Squibb where to get off. But she wouldn't, of course. Not that kind of woman. Too meek and mild for her own good.'

The other half had arrived on the counter in front of the Major and he scooped it up deftly.

'Your very good health, Colonel.'

'Thank you, Major. And yours.'

'We need it. We're neither of us getting any younger, are we? Which reminds me about Marjorie's birthday. That plant I'd chosen for her was wrecked, you know. Not sure I can face going back there to get another.'

'You could buy her something else.'

'Any ideas?'

'Try Mrs Deacon's gift shop in Dorchester.'

'She still running it?'

'Very much so.'

'I'll give it a whirl.'

After some more drinking the Colonel said, 'By the way, that woman you saw in the distance at the Manor, have you remembered anything else about her?'

The Major wagged his head. 'No. There was something that rang a bell, but I'm blessed if I can remember what it was.'

'Well, let me know if you do.'

'She wasn't the murderer, if that's what you're thinking. You didn't see the body, did you? Not like I did. Close up. Believe me, no woman could have done that to anyone. It must have been a man.'

Mrs Deacon's gift shop in Dorchester was not the sort of place the Major would normally have been seen dead in, but the fact that Marjorie's birthday was only three days away spurred him on. 'Seek and Find' it said in slanting letters above the window and the lights were on inside.

Well, that was a promising start and when he peered in through the glass the stuff for sale looked pretty good. Bound to be expensive but worth a squint round. No need to buy anything. He could be just looking.

A bell jangled as he opened the door. He rather liked that. It reminded him of the sweetshop in the village where he had lived as a child. There had been rows of big, glass, screw-top jars on shelves, full of his favourites: treacle toffees; sherbets that fizzed on your tongue and turned it yellow; long, black liquorice bootlaces; smooth, red aniseed balls; fat, striped humbugs. The man who had owned it always waited impatiently for him to make up his mind, drumming his fingers on the edge of the counter. The sweets had been weighed out on brass scales and tipped into a paper bag flipped over to twist its corners tight. Whatever the Major had chosen he often wished he'd gone for something else. Come to think of it, the same thing had kept happening in later life. The wrong path taken, the wrong door opened or shut, the wrong decision made.

Now, he found himself surrounded by pictures, lamps, vases, candlesticks, cushions, tablecloths, trays, teapots, a set of rather nice whisky glasses – and without a clue as to what might please the old girl.

'Can I help you, Major, or would you sooner just browse?'

She'd come out from behind the counter. He'd only seen Mrs Deacon once before across a crowded village hall and she was a lot more interesting close up. Quite a few years younger than her late husband. Probably somewhere in her early fifties, or even less. Younger than Tanya, that was for sure. She was wearing black clothes but they didn't look much like widows' weeds to him. Ye gods, another widow, he thought! Frog End was attracting them like flies. And how had she known who he was?

He bowed. 'Very kind of you, Mrs Deacon. The Colonel recommended your shop, you see. I'm looking for a birthday present for my wife.'

'What sort of thing do you think she might like?'

He looked around helplessly. 'Not too sure, to be honest.'

'She's a very busy woman, isn't she? Very active in the village, so I've heard.'

'Rather!'

'Then I wonder if she might like something useful like this.'

She had picked up a very smart, black, leather-bound notebook with a silver propelling pencil fitted into a slot at the side. She took out the pencil and fanned the leaves for him. They had silver edges.

'Very nice,' he said. It looked just the job for Marjorie, who was always writing things down.

'You could have her initials put on the front in silver to match, if you'd like.'

That would certainly please the old girl, he thought. Nice touch.

'Jolly good idea. I'll take it.'

He paid and they sorted out the initials (five of them, thanks to his late mother-in-law who had had delusions of grandeur). The notebook would be ready for collection the next day. She was damned efficient, he reckoned. No wonder the shop was doing well.

At the door, he paused. 'Meant to say I was very sorry about your husband, Mrs Deacon.'

She inclined her head. 'Thank you, Major.'

The bell jangled as he opened the door. He paused again.

'By the way, how did you know who I was? We've never been introduced, have we? I'd remember.'

She smiled. 'You have quite a reputation in Frog End, Major. It goes before you.'

'That so?' He closed the door behind him and squared his shoulders. By Jove, a reputation! For what exactly? Well, whatever it was, he was rather pleased.

TWELVE

'Good morning, Mrs Turner.'

'Oh . . . good morning, Colonel.'

He was raising his cap to her very politely, as he always did whenever they happened to pass each other. Once or twice he had stopped to chat when she had been pushing Johnny to or from the Manor. He was one of the few people who talked to them quite normally, always including Johnny in the conversation. Not shouting like the Major, or speaking over the top of Johnny's head as though he wasn't there, like other people did. Although, it had to be said that Johnny never made any effort to reply or to be polite. There was nothing she could do about that, unfortunately, and it was a shame because the Colonel was a kind man who meant very well – unlike some people who were just curious and often interfering. They would make stupid suggestions about things that Johnny should do to help himself – exercises, for instance, that would, apparently, soon get him walking again if he did them often enough. Nothing would ever do that, as she and Johnny both knew, but they never answered people who talked that way. It was always best to say nothing.

This time, she was walking down the Manor drive on her own, having left Johnny at the Manor to work and the Colonel was on his way up. He stopped and smiled at her.

'Mrs Harvey's very pleased to have Johnny back again.'

Somehow she had been able to persuade Johnny to change his mind. He had kept on refusing until she had started to cry and once she'd started crying she couldn't stop. He'd been very angry with her but, finally, he'd agreed to start work at the Manor again. The tears must have done it. He always hated them.

She said, 'He thought he ought to help out, seeing as Mrs Harvey's so short-handed.'

'That's very commendable. You must be very proud of your son, Mrs Turner.'

Nobody had ever said such a thing to her before. People often said that they were very sorry for Johnny, but never that there was anything to be proud of about him. And, of course, going back to work hadn't really been his idea. She swallowed.

'It's all been very hard for him, you see.'

'And for you, too.'

Unlike the Inspector, he seemed to understand, though how could he? How could anybody?

She said, 'Mrs Harvey's been very kind. She's been teaching Johnny about gardening and lending him books. It's helped such a lot.'

'From what I hear, he's getting to be a great asset at the Manor, especially now Jacob's gone.'

'Are the police still looking for Jacob?'

'I believe so.'

'Do they think he killed Mr Deacon?'

'He's definitely a suspect, I'm afraid.'

'Inspector Squibb suspected Johnny too. He told me so.'

'That's just his way of working, Mrs Turner. I wouldn't let it worry you. He likes to alarm people.'

'Anyway, Johnny couldn't have done it.'

'Of course not. As a matter of interest, though, what did your son think of Mr Deacon?'

'He didn't see very much of him. They worked in different parts of the gardens.'

The Colonel said, 'Did you know that the Deacons lost their only son in a motor bike accident many years ago?'

'No, I didn't.'

Lying was easy, once you got used to it. She could tell any number of lies for Johnny.

'I wondered if perhaps Mr Deacon had ever sympathized with your son about his own accident?'

'Johnny doesn't like talking about it to people. He wouldn't have said anything to anybody.'

'You love Johnny very much, don't you, Mrs Turner?'

'Yes.'

'You'd do anything for him, I'm sure.'

There was no need to lie this time. She said simply, 'Anything.'

He raised his cap again and she went on her way, walking quickly in order to put a safe distance between them. The Colonel had been very nice and kind but he had asked too many questions. Johnny wouldn't like that.

Alison came to stay for a weekend. The Colonel had not seen his daughter for several months. Her high-powered job kept her busy in London or on working trips abroad but she stayed in regular touch by phone.

He knew that she had worried about him since Laura had died but the fact was that he had worried even more about her. His hope had always been that she would find a good man to share her life but, as she had told him, so far it hadn't happened. She loved her job, which paid her very well, and a man would expect her to iron his shirts. Find a man who doesn't, had been his logical response but, apparently, it wasn't quite so easy. And most men expected a lot more than ironed shirts, or so his daughter had discovered. A cook, a cleaner, a nurse, for example, as well as her full and undivided attention at all times, which meant neglecting her own work.

His hopes had been raised for a while when she had spoken of 'meeting someone', but the someone in question had turned out to be a married man.

A big name in the City, Alison had told him. Living apart from his wife and with a grown-up daughter who had left home. She got on brilliantly with him, she said. They spoke the same language, enjoyed the same things and he always got his shirts done by a specialist laundry. They were taken away by invisible hands and delivered back pristine on hangers, encased in plastic. Also, the big name wanted her to move into his penthouse flat on the north bank of the river which was quite an impressive place, apparently. She hadn't mentioned the possibility of marriage and the Colonel doubted if it was in her mind, or in the big name's mind either. She was still trying to decide about the moving in.

She drove down from London on Saturday morning. On previous visits he had taken her to the Dog and Duck for lunch, but this time he had decided to cook himself. Poached salmon fillets, new potatoes and salad, and he chopped up

some parsley from the pig trough for decoration. It was all
ready and waiting by the time she arrived.

He poured glasses of white wine and they sat out on the
terrace. She looked as stylish as always in her London clothes.
There would be no country concessions to Barbours or boots
over the weekend. He wondered if she had made her decision
about the married man but knew better than to ask.

She admired the pig trough which had progressed considerably since its early days. He had added sage and chives to his
starter of parsley, as well as rosemary and thyme and Naomi's
mint and they were all doing well – the mint rather too well,
if anything.

'You're getting to be quite a gardener, Dad. Mum would be
proud of you.'

'She would have been a far better one.'

'She always wanted to live in a cottage in the country, didn't
she? I remember her talking about it.'

'That was the general idea. When we retired.'

'I thought at first it was a big mistake for you to bury
yourself down here but you've made it very nice. Don't you
get bored sometimes, though? I mean, nothing much happens,
does it?'

Frog End usually gave a false impression to people.

'You'd be surprised,' he said. 'All sorts of things go on. We
had another murder not so long ago.'

'Another one?'

'Somebody was hit over the head with a garden spade.'

'How horrible! Who?'

'A newcomer to the village. The police are investigating but
they don't seem to be able to nail the culprit.'

'They should be looking for the motive, shouldn't they?
Isn't that always the big clue? There has to be a reason. Find
it and, hey presto, you've got the answer.'

'Easier said than done.'

Thursday had appeared casually from nowhere and walked
past them. Alison was neither a cat nor a dog person and Thursday
showed that he understood this by taking a middle path – close,
but not too close.

'He's looking a bit thin, isn't he, Dad?'

'He's not eating much. I've been trying all kinds of food but he's not very interested.'

'Maybe it's old age.'

'Maybe.'

'You could take him to the vet? Get him checked over?'

He thought of his one and only visit to the surgery for a necessary inoculation and of Thursday's spitting and clawing fury, veterinary blood drawn.

'It's not quite as simple as it sounds.'

Naomi arrived to join them for the customary six o'clock drink and the subject of Lawrence Deacon's murder resurfaced.

'Your father is solving the case for us. Aren't you, Hugh?'

'Are you, Dad?'

'Not so far.'

Naomi said firmly, 'Frog End is counting on him.'

Later, he took Alison to the Dog and Duck. During the years he had known it, the pub had progressed from flagstone floors, pickled eggs and ploughman's to patterned carpeting, menus and a mock-beamed dining extension where full meals were served. Being a Saturday evening, it was busy and noisy. He had liked it much better as it had been before, but pubs, like every other business, had to move with the times.

Alison was saying something and he leaned closer to hear her better.

'By the way, I won't be moving in with the married man. In fact, I won't even be seeing him any more. It wouldn't work. And there's no need to pretend you're sorry, Dad.'

He said, 'I want you to be happy. That's all that matters.'

'Like you and Mum were?'

'Like you could be as well.'

She smiled. 'I'm happy already, Dad, thanks all the same. You don't need to worry. I'd much sooner be on my own than living with Mr Wrong and Mr Right is pretty hard to find. I don't want to settle for Mr He'll Do.'

He couldn't argue.

They went to church on Sunday morning. Matins was always well-attended in Frog End and the Colonel enjoyed singing the hymns. It was also his turn to read the second lesson – a passage from Luke that he knew well.

"'And it came to pass, when the time was come that he should be received up, he steadfastly set his face to go to Jerusalem . . .'"

The new and keen young vicar who had co-opted him both as an occasional reader and a part-time sidesman in spite of the Colonel's confessed non-belief, bounded eagerly up to the pulpit to deliver a sermon about seeds scattered on good soil always providing a plentiful harvest. The Colonel's attention drifted as the homily went on. Heads were bent. Old Mrs Watson sitting in a neighbouring pew seemed to have dropped off and the Major kept shaking his pocket watch and holding it to his ear. He noticed that Joyce Reed was present but alone, without her husband. No surprises there. Sunday Matins hadn't a great deal to offer a fanatical golfer.

The vicar finished his optimistic sermon, heads were lifted up again and the organ, with Miss Hartshorne in command at the keys, wheezed into life. The final hymn began.

Lift up your hearts! We lift them, Lord to thee . . .

The congregation had lifted themselves as well as their heads and hearts. Even Mrs Watson was on her feet and trying to find the right place in her hymnbook. It was a rousing tune and another of the Colonel's favourites, very familiar from his boarding school days. No need to look at the words.

> Here at thy feet none other may we see:
> 'Lift up your hearts!' E'en so, with one accord,
> We lift them up, we lift them to the Lord.

The Frog End congregation was making a valiant stab at it but, to his mind, so far as hymn singing was concerned, there was nothing to beat the sound of five hundred English school-boys in full-throated unison.

> Then, as the trumpet-call, in after years,
> 'Lift up your hearts!' rings pealing in our ears,
> Still shall those hearts respond, with full accord,
> 'We lift them up, we lift them to the Lord.

The Major waylaid them as they left after the service.

'Jolly good to see your daughter again, Colonel. Not often we get the pleasure.' He squeezed Alison's arm. 'You must come and cheer us up more often, my dear. This place is as dull as ditchwater.'

'It doesn't sound it. My father says there's been another murder recently.'

He dropped her arm and tapped the side of his nose. 'Best not to talk about it. Bit of a sore subject. Less said the better.'

Alison stared after his retreating back. 'What's bitten the Major? He seemed quite upset.'

'He was involved in the murder.'

'The Major? How could he possibly be?'

'He was nearby when it happened and found the body. The police gave him a bit of a grilling.'

'Poor old Major . . . still, they can't suspect him of anything, can they?'

He smiled. 'Isn't it often the least likely person?'

'That's in books, Dad.' She wagged a finger at him. 'And don't forget you're supposed to be solving the case. They're all relying on you. Look for the motive, like I said. You must be missing something. Something obvious.'

Alison left soon after lunch to drive back to London and he went and sat in the wing-back chair in the sitting room and listened to the grandfather clock tick-tocking. All the rest was silence. The silence that he still couldn't quite get used to, no matter how hard he tried. All his life there had always been other people around – his parents, his brother, his school friends, his fellow officers, Laura and the children. Now there was no one, except for Thursday who couldn't speak a word and was, in any case, usually asleep.

He got up and went over to the old gramophone that he had used for many years to play his collection of Gilbert and Sullivan records. Alison had tried to persuade him to buy some state of the art machine and modern disks but he took pleasure from handling a real old-fashioned record – admiring the cover again, sliding it from its sleeve, setting it on the turntable, pressing the switch, watching the record spin, the arm move across and descend, waiting for the music to begin.

He chose an old favourite from the stack and returned to his chair to listen.

I am the very model of a modern Major-General
I've information vegetable, animal and mineral
I know the kings of England, and I quote the fights
    historical
From Marathon to Waterloo, in order categorical . . .

As a retired Colonel, he was far from any such paragon and he certainly wasn't very modern either. His army career was past and done. His time, he accepted, was over. The things that were left to do were small things – community services, doing his bit where he could, giving a helping hand when needed, and, now it seemed, working out who had killed Lawrence Deacon. Jacob remained the chief suspect, at least as far as the police were concerned, but other than his panic-stricken flight, this case was giving no clues away. The motive was always the key, as Alison had correctly pointed out. There always had to be a reason. Jacob could well have had one, the product of his troubled mind, but who else? And what else?

I'm very good at integral and differential calculus
I know the scientific names of beings animalculous
In short, in matters vegetable, animal, and mineral
I am the very model of a modern Major-General.

Claudia Deacon? She had freely admitted to him that her marriage had cooled ever since the tragic death of the young son they never talked about any more. The lovely boy who was very special, charming, kind, good-natured, full of life and whose loss twenty years ago had virtually broken them both. But what connection could it have with Deacon's murder?

She'd told him that her husband had been very difficult to cope with since his stroke and that he resented the time she spent in her flourishing gift shop. She had also told him that her husband suspected her – wrongly, so she had said – of having an affair. But maybe he had been right? Whatever the

truth about it Claudia Deacon had had no need to murder her
husband. She could have left him at any time, if she had been
driven to such a point – of choosing between her husband and
a lover and her shop. The choices were all hers.

But perhaps Deacon's endless resentment and suspicions
had finally proved too much for his wife? Perhaps she had
simply wanted to be rid of him at any price?

What else had Claudia told him? That Deacon had apparently had no sympathy for young Johnny Turner, condemned
for the rest of his life to a wheelchair. Deacon's harsh view
had been that it had been his own fault and that he was lucky
to be alive – unlike his own son. If he had said as much to
Johnny himself then the boy might have reacted violently. He
could manoeuvre his wheelchair very well and he must have
very strong arms. Arms that could propel him and his chair
everywhere and could easily lift a heavy spade and strike a
fatal blow.

Tanya Carberry? The grieving widow, as Naomi had
described her. He had only met her once or twice – a coffee
morning, a chamber music concert in the village hall, a
gardening talk at the Manor. They hadn't exchanged more than
a few words. All he knew was that her husband had died very
suddenly, soon after they had moved into their flat at the Hall,
and that she had been doing occasional work at the Manor to
help her get over depression. Naomi had voiced the rather
farfetched theory that widows always attracted men and that
Deacon had tried his luck. He couldn't see that happening.
Mrs Carberry was a good-looking woman but she was clearly
still in mourning for her husband and would be far from
grateful for the attention. In any case, Deacon had been a sick
man, very much preoccupied with his own misfortune.

Which brought him to the Major, who had stumbled on the
scene of the crime. So far, nobody had seriously thought of
him as a possible suspect. The idea was ridiculous and had
been dismissed by everyone, even Inspector Squibb – blood-
spattered blazer notwithstanding. Marjorie Cuthbertson, he felt
sure, would share the view that her husband was quite incapable
of murdering anyone. And she should know.

There was, of course, always the possibility that the murderer

had been a complete stranger to Frog End. An outsider passing
through and wandering freely around the Manor gardens, as
visitors often did. There were plenty of unstable people at
large these days. People who killed for some imagined reason,
or for none at all. Or perhaps it had been someone who had
known Deacon in the past? An old enemy who had finally
tracked him down to take revenge? The Colonel knew that he
was straying into the realms of fantasy but one had only to
pick up a daily newspaper to read about true happenings that
were far stranger than fiction.

One thing was sure, whoever had killed Deacon would have
had enough strength to strike fatal blows. There had been no
risking a half-done job.

Then I can write a washing bill in Babylonic cuneform
And tell you ev'ry detail of Caractacus's uniform
In short, in matters vegetable, animal and mineral
I am the very model of a modern Major-General

The phone rang and the Colonel lifted the receiver.
Ruth said, 'They've found Jacob.'

THIRTEEN

The police had found Jacob cowering in an overgrown hollow deep in woods beyond Frog End. Their dogs had tracked him down like an animal. He had been arrested and taken to the police station. The Harveys' solicitor had been present to see fair play but the Colonel had been denied any access to Jacob. Inspector Squibb had remained adamant.

'He's being held in a cell for questioning, sir.'

'On what charge?'

'None, as yet.'

'How long is he to be held?'

'At least twenty-four hours. Longer, if we have reason to suspect him of a serious crime, such as murder – which we do.'

'What evidence do you have?'

'More than sufficient.'

'Jacob's fingerprints may be on the murder weapon, Inspector, but that's not proof. According to Mrs Harvey, he used the same spade many times for his work at the Manor. Fingerprints can last a long time, I believe.'

'As Frog End's amateur sleuth, Colonel, perhaps you can also explain away the blood belonging to Mr Deacon left on the Major's blazer lapel?'

'Jacob must have touched Mr Deacon's body when he discovered it. It would have been a natural reaction. He might also have touched the spade.'

'He might also have picked it up and hit Mr Deacon very hard over the head. Otherwise, why did he run off? And keep running? And hiding?'

'He was probably afraid that he would be suspected.'

'With good reason. But what was he doing in the greenhouse in the first place? I'd like to know. According to Mrs Harvey, he was meant to be digging over a potato patch in the kitchen garden.'

'Have you asked him?'

'Many times. He won't say. In fact, he won't say anything – or nothing that I can understand.'

'Mrs Harvey thinks he may have gone to the greenhouse because he was worried about Mr Deacon pinching out the tomatoes. It was usually his job.'

'So she told me. Which makes it all the more likely that he killed Lawrence Deacon.'

'Over tomato side shoots?'

'Jacob's a nutcase, Colonel, and nutcases don't think or behave like normal people. And don't forget he resented Mr Deacon being there at all. Saw him as a threat.'

'That's supposition, Inspector. We don't know for certain how Jacob felt about him, or what he thinks about anything, for that matter. If you'd let me talk with him I might be able to get some proper answers.'

Jacob trusts me, he might have added, except that it was impossible to claim any such thing. More likely, Jacob trusted nobody.

The Inspector opened his office door. 'That won't be necessary, thank you, sir. We don't need to use up any more of your valuable time.'

The Colonel paused as he left the room. 'I doubt if Jacob would ever be considered fit to plead, Inspector.'

'That's not for us to decide, is it, Colonel?'

Sheila was late collecting Johnny but it was all right because he was still busy doing the watering. Sheila waited until he'd finished and watched while he wound up the hose, quick and neat as anything. The way he managed the chair these days was a marvel. Spinning it round on a sixpence, taking corners in one, whipping forwards and backwards along narrow paths. Such a difference from when he'd started and had refused even to lay a finger on the wheels. Now, as long as the surface was reasonably smooth and flat, he could go anywhere, not to mention that Dr and Mrs Harvey had now provided special ramps for disabled visitors wherever they were needed. It wasn't quite so easy in some places, of course. That's where she came in. Johnny still needed her for the tricky bits. She still had a role to play. And everything was going to work out, now that Mr Deacon had gone. She'd booked her first driving lesson with Never Fail already.

'I'm ready, Mum.'

He seemed in a much better mood – not cross with her any more. She pushed the chair down the drive quite fast. The days of aching arms and painful blisters had passed and the sun was shining.

Johnny said, 'Mrs Harvey says the police have found Jacob.'

She stopped pushing. 'Where was he?'

'Hiding in some woods. They've arrested him. He's being questioned about the murder of Mr Deacon. He didn't do it, though.'

'How do you know he didn't, Johnny?'

'Because Jacob's not like that.'

'You can't be sure. Not with someone like him.'

'Yes, I can, Mum. I've learned a lot about people. You do when you're in a wheelchair. You watch people when they're not watching you. They don't see you properly because you don't count as normal for them. But you notice things about them all the time – things that nobody else notices. It wasn't Jacob. They've got the wrong person.'

She dared not ask any more questions. Instead, she carried on in silence, pushing the wheelchair down the gravel driveway, out of the Manor gates, round the green and down the slope to The Close. As they passed Shangri-La the Major came to the window and raised a half-empty glass.

On his way back from the police station, the Colonel stopped at the Manor. He found Ruth upstairs, bathing his godson. She was cradling him carefully in the warm water and Alan was splashing about with his arms and kicking hard with his legs.

'He loves it,' Ruth said. 'Float the duck towards him, will you, Hugh.'

The bright yellow plastic duck bobbed along merrily and the baby grabbed hold of its orange beak and stuffed it in his mouth.

The Colonel thought of bath times long ago when Marcus and Alison had been very small and Laura had been in charge.

There had been other ducks and boats and fish floating about and a green turtle with a hollow back for holding soap which had been a particular favourite. After bath time there had always been a bedtime story or nursery rhymes which he had enjoyed reading to the children. *King John was not a good man, he had his little ways, and sometimes no one spoke to him for days and days and days . . .* He could still remember the words and feeling sorry for the king who had no friends and sent himself Christmas cards.

Army duties had often meant missing out on such pleasures and later, when he had been posted abroad to outlandish places and Marcus and Alison had been sent to boarding schools in England, he and Laura had both missed out on a great deal more. So, he thought regretfully, had the children.

He said, 'I'm afraid I didn't get very far with Inspector Squibb. He wouldn't let me near Jacob.'

'Tom only saw him for a moment. He says he was in a dreadful state. I wish we could help him.'

'The police are a long way from actually proving anything. The fingerprints on the spade handle could well be old ones.'

'What about the blood he left on the Major's blazer?'

'Jacob must have got it on his hands when he found Deacon's body.'

'The Major seems convinced that he's guilty.'

'The Major saw him running out of the greenhouse in a panic, that's all.'

Ruth said, 'Well, if Jacob didn't kill Lawrence, it must have been someone else.'

The duck was bobbing about in the bath again. The Colonel re-directed it back to his godson. Freda Butler had made the same very logical remark. And like Miss Butler, Ruth was waiting for him to come up with something helpful. Something comforting. At the moment, he had nothing to say, but he still had something to do. It was high time to visit Tanya Carberry and find out more about her.

When the flat doorbell rang, Tanya was afraid that Inspector Squibb had come to interview her again. More than afraid, she was petrified. She waited, unmoving, and after a moment or two the bell rang again. It didn't sound like the Inspector. His ring had been loud and peremptory whereas this one was quiet and polite. If it was someone from one of the other flats they might think her unfriendly or rude if she didn't answer. After waiting another moment, she went to the door and opened it.

'Good evening, Mrs Carberry. I'm so sorry to disturb you.'

She had met him once or twice and seen him at the Manor several times. He was a good friend of the Harveys and a godfather to little Alan, which meant that he was to be trusted.

'Please come in, Colonel.'

In the sitting room, she invited him to sit down. He did so, smiling at her. It was a very charming, reassuring smile.

'I'll come straight to the point and I promise I won't keep you long.'

What a contrast to the Inspector, she thought.

'What can I do for you, Colonel?'

'I'm sure you'll have heard that Jacob has been found and arrested by the police and that he's suspected of murdering Lawrence Deacon?'

'It's not surprising, is it? Considering the circumstances.'

'They are rather damning, I agree, but although the circumstances point towards Jacob's guilt there is no actual proof of it at all.'

'There was blood on his hands. Major Cuthbertson said so.'

'Nevertheless, Dr and Mrs Harvey don't believe that he's guilty. Nor do I. It's not in his nature to attack anyone and we firmly believe that he's innocent. So, I was wondering, Mrs Carberry, if you could add anything to the picture that might help us establish his innocence, or at least throw some doubt on his guilt.'

She said, 'I'm sorry but I've nothing more to say. I've already been interviewed by Inspector Squibb at considerable length.'

'So I gather. And I'm sure it wasn't a pleasant experience for you.'

'No, it wasn't.'

'I'll try to do better. Could we go over the events on that

day very briefly – if it wouldn't be too much for you? I'll leave at once, if you prefer.'

She said, 'I really don't see how I can help you.'

'It's just a question of checking the facts. Making quite sure of them. I believe you were working on one of the herbaceous borders when you heard Major Cuthbertson shouting for help?'

She nodded. 'I ran over and found him standing outside the greenhouse door in a state of shock. He told me that there was a body inside. I didn't believe him at first but when I went to look I saw Mr Deacon lying there face down.'

'You knew it was him?'

'I recognized his clothes. As I told Inspector Squibb, he always wore the same ones for work.' She shuddered. 'There was a great deal of blood. At first, I thought he must have had another stroke and injured himself as he fell . . . until I went nearer and saw the spade.'

'You were aware that he was working there that morning?'

She nodded. 'He'd come by the border earlier and told me he'd been given the chore of pinching out the tomato side shoots. He said he was taking a break as it was very boring.'

'Did he say anything else to you?'

'No.'

'Nothing offensive or upsetting?'

'No. Just about the tomatoes.'

'What did he do then?'

'He walked off – back to work in the greenhouse, I assume. I really don't know. I'd prefer not to talk about this any more, if you don't mind, Colonel.'

He said, 'I'm very sorry to distress you, Mrs Carberry. There was a reason for my question. If Mr Deacon was ever offensive to you in any way, then he could also have offended others. I understand from his wife that he could be quite a difficult man. He may have done or said something that led to his murder. Somebody had a very strong reason for killing him.'

'Jacob did. Mr Deacon treated him unkindly. He taunted him.'

'Jacob's odd, but he's never been violent. He shies away from people and avoids any sort of trouble. Inspector Squibb wrongly believes him to be guilty and poor Jacob isn't capable of defending himself. That's why I'm standing up for him. I need your help, if you're willing to give it.'

She was silent for a moment. At last, she said, 'Lawrence Deacon pretended to be nice, but he wasn't. He told me once that his wife was having an affair. I wouldn't have blamed her if it was true but I think he made it up.'

'Why do you think that?'

'I went to Mrs Deacon's shop in Dorchester when I was trying to find a present for someone. She didn't seem at all the sort of person who would be interested in having an affair. I could tell that her shop meant a lot to her and that she was very proud of it. Her husband seemed to resent that.'

'Did he say so to you?'

'He said that there was no need for her to work. She could have stayed at home with him.'

'Is there anything else you can tell me about Mr Deacon?'

'He was horrible to Johnny, as well. I overheard him telling him that he was glad that he would never be able to walk again. That it served him right.'

'What did Johnny say?'

'Nothing. He didn't answer.'

'He must have been upset or angry?'

'I don't know. He just went away.'

'Did you say anything about this to Inspector Squibb?'

'No. I didn't want to get Johnny into any trouble. He's suffered enough. Besides, he couldn't have had anything to do with the murder.'

'What makes you think that?'

'He can't walk, can he? How could he possibly have killed Mr Deacon?'

'From what I've seen, Johnny is very adept at getting about in his wheelchair, and he has extremely strong arms. Haven't you noticed?'

She stared at him. 'Well, he didn't do it, Colonel. I'm quite sure of it.'

'Where was he on the day of the murder?'

'Working in the rose garden, I think. I didn't actually see him until he came up to the greenhouse after the Major had discovered Mr Deacon's body.'

'You didn't see him before then – at any time during the day?'

'No.'

'Not at all?'

'No. Not at all.'

'I understand he often came to eat his lunchtime sandwiches with you at the old stables?'

'He did sometimes but I wouldn't say it was often.'

'What did you talk about?'

'He never said much.'

'Not even about his accident?'

'He never talked about it and I would never have raised the subject. It was a terrible thing to happen and it had obviously affected him deeply.'

'Mrs Harvey told me he was doing well with the gardening. Learning a lot and getting rather interested.'

'She was very kind to him and lent him books.'

'And now he's back at work again.'

'Yes, Mrs Harvey's very pleased.'

'Does he still have his sandwiches with you?'

'Not since the murder.'

The Colonel said, 'Going back to that day, what did Johnny do when he arrived at the greenhouse?'

'There was nothing he could do. I suppose he must have waited around until his mother came to take him home. I really can't remember. It's all a blur.' She put her hand to her forehead. 'I'd like you to go now, if you don't mind. I've got a dreadful headache.'

He left at once. When she had closed the door, she leaned against it. She'd told him the truth, but not the whole truth.

The Major was considering the whisky glass in his hand. It was either half-full or half-empty, depending on which way you saw things. The trick was to keep an open mind and let life jog along with its ups and downs – more downs than ups these days, it seemed to him. He still hadn't got his best blazer back and he was still shaky from seeing Deacon's body prone among the tomatoes. What a horrible sight! And all that blood! It would probably haunt him until the end of his days.

He held out his other hand in front of him to see if it was still shaking. Yes, a definite tremor. You could tell a lot about people's state of mind from their hands – whether they were nervous, or angry, or tense or, as in his own case, suffering from delayed shock. Hands were symbolic, of course. You gave someone a helping hand, you shook their hand to seal a bargain, or to extend a welcome. Fathers gave their daughters' hands in marriage – Marjorie's father, a major general, had been noticeably reluctant, as he remembered. People waved hallo and goodbye with their hands, clapped them together to applaud, put thumbs up or down to show approval or otherwise. And not forgetting, of course, Winston Churchill's famous V-sign for victory with his hand. Now, there was a real leader of men! If it hadn't been for Churchill, people would have thrown in their towels instead of bagging sun beds and everyone would be speaking German now.

He drank some more whisky and looked at the glass again. More like half-empty now, and when he looked a bit more closely he could see chips on the rim and smears all over the glass – the old girl's idea of washing-up. In the old days, serving abroad, they'd always had servants who knew what they were doing. The glasses had always shone brightly. No chips or spots or smears. The one he was holding was the last survivor from the expensive set the regiment had given him for his retirement, along with the musical cocktail cabinet. The rest of them had long since bitten the dust, thanks to Marjorie's kitchen ministrations.

Time to get some new ones. No question. But where from? And then he remembered seeing a whole set of whisky glasses in Claudia Deacon's shop. Damned nice-looking ones too. It would mean another visit to Seek and Find which was rather a good idea, when he thought about it.

Later, over supper, he put it boldly to the old girl while he was trying to identify whatever she'd cooked. Some kind of fish, he thought, in which case he had to watch out for bones. Lethal, if you didn't. They could stick in the throat and choke you to death. He poked around with his fork. Yes, it was fish all right. Haddock, probably. Or hake. Or cod. They all tasted

the same. He manoeuvred a sharp white bone carefully on
to the side of his plate.

'I've been thinking that we ought to get some more glasses,
Marjorie.'

'What for? We've got a cupboard full of them.'

'They're not for whisky.'

Among the many things that his wife had never understood
was whisky glasses and what they should be like. Heavy
bottomed, good to hold and good to look at.

'You've got a perfectly good glass already, Roger.'

'There's a chip on the rim – I nearly cut my lip on it this
evening.'

'You shouldn't drink so fast.'

He said with dignity, 'I'd like to get some new ones, if you
don't mind. I'll pay for them, of course.'

She sighed. 'If you insist.'

He had discovered another fishbone and steered it over to
join the first. 'I noticed some in that gift shop in Dorchester
where I bought the notebook for your birthday.'

'Mrs Deacon's place?'

'As it happens.'

'I thought it might be. Don't start getting any of your ideas,
Roger. You know they always land you in trouble.'

'I don't know what you mean.'

'Yes, you do, but never mind. And don't go spending a
fortune. They'll only get broken.'

Which was true enough. He might as well go to that shop
in the town where everything cost a pound. Except that some
things in life still mattered and drinking a decent whisky out
of a decent glass was one of them. The set he'd noticed in
Seek and Find had looked just the job and he reckoned he'd
earned them, what with all the fetching and carrying and
waiting around that he had to put up with every day of what
remained of his life.

'I'll go tomorrow,' he said.

The Major took some trouble over his appearance for re-visiting
Seek and Find. The second-best blazer would have to do in
lieu of the best one, still held in police custody. Not that he

wanted it back now. The mere thought made him shudder. He
donned a double-cuffed white shirt from one of those places
in Jermyn Street, put in his monogrammed silver cufflinks and
tied his old regimental tie. A last check in the long mirror
assured him that everything was tickety-boo. He peered closer
and smoothed his hair. Not quite so much of it on top, maybe,
but a lot more than most older men – except the Colonel. It was
all in the genes, so they said. Handed down from generation to
generation and not much you could do about it. He turned sideways for a different view of his reflection. According to Claudia,
as he now called her in his mind, he had a reputation. It went
before him, apparently. She hadn't said what the reputation was
for, but in his book, it could only mean one thing. If the Major
had had moustaches, he might have twirled them but he contented
himself with shooting his cuffs.

Things had not been going quite as smoothly with Tanya
as he'd hoped. She was always too busy to talk to him when
she was working at the Manor and he was beginning to ask
himself if she was worth the time and trouble he was taking.
There were other fish in the sea, though not so many these
days, it was true. On balance, it was probably still better to
hang on. Stick to his course. Go on playing the game. But
now that the fête was over he'd have to think up another excuse
for calling at the Manor.

He backed the Escort out of the garage, no trouble at all
– the old girl rarely missed a gatepost – and breezed off towards
Dorchester, one arm on the wheel. Sometimes – but not very
often – he felt quite young again.

The bell jangled as he opened the door to Seek and Find,
bringing back the old sweet shop memories. Humbugs, he
thought wistfully. That's what he'd choose today, if he could.
And maybe some treacle toffees – if only the old gnashers
were still up to it.

To his annoyance, he wasn't the only customer. Some woman
was already at the counter, talking and trying to choose between
two almost identical flower vases and he could tell from bitter
experience that she was going to dither for a long time. What
was it about women? If men had something to say and decide

they said it and decided. That was the end of it. Finished and done.

He had a look round for the whisky glasses. No sign of them.

'Can I help you, Major?'

Another woman had come up behind him while he was searching. Who the hell was she?

'I'm Mrs Deacon's assistant. She's rather busy at the moment. Is there anything I can do for you?'

He hadn't realized that Claudia had anybody to help her. Plain as a pikestaff, he noted, or he might have taken up the offer. He wondered if she had heard about his reputation too?

He said firmly, 'No, thank you. I'll wait until Mrs Deacon's free.'

She went off to the back of the shop and he wandered around a bit more, looking in vain for the glasses. The customer at the counter had finally made up her mind after changing it several times, but now she had started complaining about her husband. On and on she was going about how he always took her for granted. She was damn lucky to have one at all, he thought. The assistant had been a pikestaff, but this one was a battleaxe. If she were his wife, he'd have got rid of her long ago.

Another ten minutes went by before the woman finally paid for the chosen vase and left with much loud and unnecessary jangling of the sweet-shop doorbell. No consideration for others, he thought. None at all. But that was the way it went these days. Nobody gave a damn any more.

'I'm so sorry you've been kept waiting, Major. I'm afraid some of my customers like to take their time. I have to be patient. It's all part of the job.' She was smiling at him. 'I hoped Edie might be able to help you.'

'Edie?'

'My assistant. She works here on Thursdays and Saturdays.'

Claudia was even better looking than he remembered. A mature woman, of course, but none the worse for that. He'd always preferred them himself, especially now he was getting on a bit. They knew how many beans made five, whatever it was. He couldn't cope with the young ones any more. Couldn't understand what they were saying, for one thing.

'Actually, I wanted a word with you.'

'Well, now that I'm free, what can I do for you, Major?'

He explained about the whisky glasses. 'I happened to notice them when I was in last time, buying the present for my wife.'

'Oh yes, the notebook and pencil. I hope she liked it.'

'It was a jolly good idea of yours,' he said. 'Marjorie's not easy to please.'

'And now you're looking for some whisky glasses for her?'

'Not for her. For me. You had a set of six. Out on a table somewhere.'

'I'm very sorry, Major, but I sold them the day before yesterday.'

He felt crushed out of all proportion. They were only modern glasses, after all, not golden tankards from some pharaoh's tomb. But he'd liked the look of them and he'd already got used to the idea of owning them. Had pictured himself taking one from the cocktail cabinet, pouring a good-sized measure, retreating to his fireside chair and raising it – chipless and glinting before his eyes. The whisky would taste all the better, like wine from crystal and tea from bone china.

Claudia Deacon said, 'But I do have another set, very similar to the ones you saw. They've only just come in. Would you like to see them?'

He waited anxiously until she came back with a very smart-looking box and opened it for him. He lifted a glass out, weighing it in his hand, holding it up to the light and running his fingertip round the rim. It passed the tests with flying colours. Heavy bottomed, good to look at and good to feel. And there were six of them. Even allowing for Marjorie's rate of attrition, they should keep him going for a while. They cost a fair bit, as he discovered, but he paid up like a man. They were worth it.

He waited while she stowed the box in a strong carrier bag. Now would be the very moment to ask her to join him for a thank-you drink, considering that she'd been so helpful, not once but twice. There was a quiet little bar he knew of not too far away, and Whatshername could hold the fort.

'Here you are, Major. I do hope you enjoy using them.'

She was holding out the carrier bag and he was just about

to pop the drink question to her when the shop bell jangled loudly again and a customer came in. Another woman and, from the look and sound of her, she was going to be as inconsiderate as the one before. No good hanging around any longer. He could wait for hours.

He popped into the quiet little bar, nevertheless, and had a couple of quick ones before he drove back to Frog End. To his relief, Marjorie was out. It was her turn for doing the font flowers, he remembered, which would take some time. Competition among the village ladies over the church flowers was always cutthroat, but the font display, he had learned, counted the most. The altar and chancel vases might impress with their towering and colourful arrangements but the ancient Norman font, still in its original position by the west window after more than six hundred years, caught the eye on entering the church and was generally felt to require a more subtle approach. Surprisingly, the old girl was a match for it. Her all-white effort last Easter had been praised to the skies.

He unpacked the new glasses and put them carefully away in the cocktail cabinet, accompanied by 'Drink to Me Only'. Right on cue his late mother-in-law's clock chimed six silvery pings from the mantelpiece. He poured a celebratory measure into one of the glasses and took it back to his armchair. A toast was in order, though he couldn't think of one for a moment. Finally, with Dusty Coleman in mind, and others who had preceded him, he raised his brand-new glass to absent friends.

Too bad about Claudia, but there would always be another chance. He could visit the shop on any excuse and ask her out again. She was bound to accept, he thought, given his reputation.

FOURTEEN

'The grand draw takes place this Saturday, Colonel.'

'Draw?'

Miss Butler had just happened to be passing by his front gate as he had opened the door on his way out. He had no idea what she was talking about.

'For the Greenfields Animal Shelter raffle prizes. You very kindly bought a whole book of tickets. You will be notified, of course, if you are one of the lucky winners.'

He smiled. 'I never win, Miss Butler. I told you.'

'But I do so hope that you do this time. Perhaps not the first prize, but the second or third.'

'I'm afraid I can't remember what they are.'

'First prize is a week's holiday for two at a luxury hotel in Barcelona, Spain.' Miss Butler's cheeks turned pink. 'I don't think that would be quite right for you, Colonel. But you might enjoy the case of English sparkling wine, or the willow basket of sun-ripened fruit.'

'We'll wait and see what happens, shall we?'

'I'll be present at the draw myself and keeping my fingers crossed for you.'

'Thank you.'

She came a little closer to the gate.

'I've been wondering if you've made any progress, Colonel?'

'Progress?'

'About Mr Deacon's murderer? I know the police have arrested Jacob, but I really don't believe he would have done it, do you? It's not in his nature.'

'No, it's not.'

'Mrs Carberry still seems the most likely suspect, in my opinion. We know so little about her, don't we? She's very new to the village.'

'I'm afraid I don't think that she did it either.'

'Oh dear, I was hoping that perhaps she had. What about

Mrs Deacon, herself? She must have got very tired of her husband being an invalid, especially with her busy shop to run. Some gentlemen can be rather difficult, can't they?'

Miss Butler's father, the late Admiral, had probably provided her with plenty of first-hand experience of difficult gentlemen.

'Rather a drastic solution, though.'

'I suppose so.' Miss Butler sighed. 'It's all very unsettling, isn't it? Johnny might be another possibility – if he could walk, but he can't, so he couldn't, and anyway I can't imagine why he'd want to kill Mr Deacon. What good would it do? Poor, poor young man. I feel so sorry for him not able to enjoy life like other young men. Tragic! And I pity his poor mother having to push him everywhere in that wheelchair, as though he were a baby. It must be awful for them both. Humiliating for him and such hard work for her. I've watched her struggling along and I've often wondered how on earth she manages, being so frail herself. But, of course, she does it for Johnny and that's what's given her the strength. Luckily she seems to find it easier now. Practice makes perfect, doesn't it, Colonel?'

'It can certainly help.'

'That's why athletes train so hard, of course. The sad thing is that Johnny had been so much brighter and better lately and Dr Harvey's gardening therapy idea was getting to be such a success. Such a breakthrough! Mrs Turner must have had high hopes for him. But after Mr Deacon was murdered and the police interviewed Johnny, he refused to go back to the Manor. I'm not at all surprised, are you? Inspector Squibb is enough to upset anyone. I wish he'd just go away and leave Frog End alone.'

'He will. Don't worry, Miss Butler.'

'I can't stop worrying, I'm afraid.' She hooked her handbag further up her arm. 'Of course, there's always Mrs Reed. We don't know much about her either. And still less about her husband. Nobody in Frog End has ever seen him – not even me – which is rather strange, don't you think? Very puzzling.'

The *U-Bootwaffe* binoculars housed at the ready in the bureau drawer had not been mentioned but they were obviously uppermost in Miss Butler's mind.

'He's very keen on his golf.'

'Yes, but husbands have to come home at night, don't they? They need to go to sleep somewhere. And how does he get to and from his golf when they only seem to have the one car? Mrs Reed's health wouldn't be up to chauffeuring him, would it?'

'Perhaps somebody from his club gives him a lift.'

Miss Butler looked doubtful. 'It's possible, I suppose. He certainly seems to play a great deal. All day and every day, so far as I can see, wherever it is. I know Mrs Thompson's husband enjoys an occasional game locally – when he has the time – but it's only a small nine-hole course and she says Mr Reed definitely doesn't play there. He must belong to a club with a much bigger course, considering what an excellent player he must be, with all those silver cups. I wonder which club it is?'

'It has eighteen holes, according to Mrs Reed.'

'That sounds a lot.'

'I believe it's quite normal.'

'If you say so, Colonel. I'm sure you know all about these things. I've been thinking of something else, too. We only have Mrs Reed's word for it that she wasn't at the Manor on that terrible day. She may not have actually been working there but she could still have gone there, couldn't she? Unfortunately, I wasn't actually at home myself, so I can't be sure whether she left the Hall or not. But I've heard that the Major happened to notice a woman while he was trying to choose his plant. He was standing by the benches when he looked up and saw her in the distance.'

The Frog End grapevine was clearly on top form.

He said, 'I'm afraid he only saw her for a moment. Not clearly enough to identify her.'

'So I understand. Such a pity that the Major's sight isn't better or we might have the answer to our mystery. He really should wear stronger spectacles, but gentlemen can be rather vain about such things. My late father was always bumping into the furniture yet he maintained to the end that he had perfect vision.' Another tug on the handbag which had slithered back down her arm 'Well, I mustn't keep you any longer,

Colonel. I'm sure you're very busy. Perhaps we'll have some news from the Inspector soon.'

He stood in his doorway, watching her go and thinking about what she had said.

It was a great shame that Miss Butler had never met the U-boat captain who must have scanned his North Atlantic quite as assiduously as she monitored her Frog End village green. Every wave and every blade between them. They would have made a striking partnership. The German in his piratical white captain's cap, a Führer-awarded black iron cross sported at his neck and several days' growth of beard. Miss Butler, ultra-neat and restrained in English navy blue, her hat on her head, her handbag hooked over her arm. He doubted that there was much that the captain could have taught Miss Butler about wielding a pair of powerful Zeiss binoculars to maximum effect, but he would have held all the aces when it came to commanding his boat. Submariners were tough men – they had to be – and none tougher than their captain who couldn't afford the least sign of weakness or fear. Yes, it was a great pity that the captain and Miss Butler had never met.

It was the Colonel's turn to take old Mrs Pennyfeather to hospital for her weekly exercise class. This was never less than a pleasure because she was always interesting. The journey there and the journey back were full of Mrs Pennyfeather's views on a very long life and covered all aspects of her experience. She had seen world wars come and go, dictators live and die, kings succeed queens and the other way round – one of them abdicating inexcusably in her opinion – and countries rise and fall. She held strong opinions about most things and about most people and reserved her deepest contempt for politicians of all kinds. In her view, they were cowards, liars and cheats. The only exception was Winston Churchill.

'Worth all the rest put together,' she had told the Colonel many times.

She occasionally re-lived the time of Dunkirk when her husband had been taken prisoner of war and she had had to wait more than six months to learn if he was dead or alive. German troops had apparently unearthed him in a French farmhouse cellar, drinking it dry. Thereafter he had languished in a prison camp in Poland for five long years.

'After VE Day they flew him home in a Lancaster with a lot of other POWs. He was just like a wild dog, you know. Not a civilized bone left in his body. It had all been about survival, you see. Staying alive somehow. Nothing else had mattered. I nearly gave up on him but it was all right in the end.'

It was hard to imagine Mrs Pennyfeather giving up on anything if her determination with her arm was anything to go by. An awkward fall on slippery ground had resulted in a multiple break. The shattered bones had been reassembled in hospital with the aid of a metal plate and screws, followed up by many hours of remedial exercises. The Colonel knew that she had attended every session faithfully and practised the exercises at home.

As he settled her in the front passenger seat, she stuck out the arm for his inspection.

'What do you think of it now, eh, Colonel? I reckon I could out-wrestle you any day of the week.'

He thought it more than likely. The arm, which had been reduced to a thin white stick when he had first seen it, now looked strong and healthy. Practice had made perfect, as Miss Butler had once quite rightly observed.

He drove Mrs Pennyfeather rather faster than he drove his other elderly passengers and she entertained him with her thoughts on the present state of the world which she considered shocking. Cruelty, greed, dishonesty; sometimes she didn't think it was worth making the considerable effort to stay alive much longer. She'd given up watching TV news, she told him, especially the BBC's which was always so depressing, and anyway she couldn't hear or understand what the readers were saying.

'Nobody speaks clearly any more, haven't you noticed?'

As a matter of fact, he had. He'd put it down to his own hearing deteriorating and wondered whether that was also Mrs Pennyfeather's problem. It was difficult to tell exactly how old she was – somewhere in her mid-nineties, he guessed. A survivor from an indomitable age.

She leaned across.

'Can't you make this old rattletrap go any faster, Colonel?'

He put his foot down to take the Riley briskly up a steep hill. Mrs Pennyfeather wound down her window and let the wind blow her hair about. Just for a moment, sitting beside him, she seemed to him more like nineteen than ninety.

'Fast enough for you?' he asked.

'I suppose it'll have to do.'

'Hallo, Father. How are you?'

'Very well, thank you, Susan. How are you all?'

'Edith's had another cold but she's almost over it, I'm thankful to say. Are you keeping fit?'

'Reasonably so.'

'No aches and pains?'

'No more than usual.'

'And you're eating properly?'

'I think so.'

'Taking your vitamin pills?'

'Yes, indeed.'

So far there had been no mention of any bungalows for sale.

'I've been expecting you to call us, Father. About your visit. We need to finalize it.'

Damn it! He'd forgotten that the school holidays would have begun. It was hard to keep track of them. The terms seemed so short now and the half-terms so long. Nothing like in the old days when it had been the other way round.

'I'm looking forward to it very much.'

Diary pages rustled.

'We're getting quite booked up already but we'll be free at the end of next week. You could come then.'

He said, 'I'm very sorry, Susan, but I won't be able to manage that. Things are rather busy here at the moment.'

'Busy?'

He appreciated that it would be hard to understand, given his circumstances.

'I'm involved with a local problem that has to be sorted out.'

'Can't someone else deal with it?'

'I'm afraid not. People are relying on me.'

'Oh, I see.' She clearly didn't. 'Well, when can you come?'

'I'll make it just as soon as I can.'

'The children will be very disappointed, Father. Especially Eric. He's been looking forward to seeing you.'

'I'll do my best to make it up to him, I promise. Take him out on a special treat of his own.'

With any luck they might be able to do the old bomber airfields in Norfolk after all.

'It would be much better if we all went somewhere together, otherwise Edith will feel left out.'

He knew when he was batting on a losing wicket.

'Just as you like.'

'We could visit Littleland.'

'Littleland?'

'It's a model English village with quaint old cottages and a church and a farm, all in perfect miniature, just a few feet high. It's only been open for a few months. We haven't been there yet but it's said to be very popular with small children and to have full parental approval. Edith would love it.'

The bomber airfields were receding rapidly. Control towers, Nissen huts, perimeter tracks, old runways vanishing into the mist.

'Perhaps Eric would sooner do something else with me . . . I'll have a word with him and see if he's got any ideas.'

'I'm afraid he can't be trusted to be sensible these days, Father. He'd suggest something quite unsuitable. Littleland would be much safer for us all.' The pages rustled again. 'You'll let me know as soon as your local problem is solved, won't you, so we can arrange a firm date?'

'Yes,' he said. 'I don't think it will be long now.'

He went out into the garden to check on the general progress. The pig trough was doing well, the mint brought under control so that there was room for all, as originally intended. He moved on to the border to admire the lupins, the foxgloves and the delphiniums in their full summer colour and glory, and stopped to give an encouraging word to Miss Jekyll with her pretty sky-blue flowers who seemed very content in the sunny spot he had chosen for her. Thursday was following him, as he often did, and he walked slowly so that the old cat could keep up. They paused at the pond, and the Colonel sat down on the bench, Thursday lying close beside him. The six goldfish were all still present and correct and circling hopefully but, for once, Thursday showed no more interest in them than he did in the tins of gourmet cat food. The Tempting Terrine of Salmon, the Duck Delight, the Grilled Fish Medley had all been ignored lately.

The Colonel went on watching the fish for a while, his thoughts elsewhere.

If Tanya Carberry were to be believed – and he saw no reason why she wasn't – Deacon had positively encouraged people to hit him over the head with a spade. And the prerequisite for that action was not only a strong motive, but also the physical strength to do it hard enough to be sure to kill him. Nothing less would do.

Miss Butler's comments about Joyce Reed's husband had been very much to the point. No one in Frog End, it seemed, had ever laid eyes on him, not even Miss Butler herself on duty at her sitting-room window. It was more than puzzling, it was unbelievable.

The next day the Colonel visited two eighteen-hole golf clubs, both within a reasonable distance of Frog End. Neither, he soon discovered, had a member named Arthur Reed. At the second, though, he was lucky enough to run into a very helpful and friendly club secretary who invited him to watch the players in action on one of the greens close to the club house. The Colonel admired the civilized pace of the game, the ritual courtesy between the players, the air of calm so often lacking in other sports. It was certainly appealing but, for some reason, he had never felt any wish to play golf himself. His loss, very probably, but it was rather late now to change his ways. He was not, and never would be, a golfing man.

'We're not quite Sunningdale here yet,' the secretary told him, 'but I think you'd find this a very pleasant club.'

The Colonel said, 'I don't doubt it, but I'm afraid I'm here under false pretences. I'm not looking for a club to join. I'm trying to find a man who belongs to one somewhere in Dorset.'

'Well, if you'd care to give me his name, I might be able to help you. I'm familiar with most of the local players.'

'It's Arthur Reed.'

'That's interesting.'

'Do you know him?'

'Quite well, actually. Or I used to. He was a pretty good club player, though we can't lay claim to him here in Dorset. Hampshire's his home ground – or was, before he moved away.'

'As a matter of fact, he and his wife have bought a flat in the Dorset village where I live.'

'Have you ever met him?'

'No, I can't say that I have.'

'I would have been surprised if you had. He walked out on his wife when they were living in Hampshire and went off with someone else's wife from the same club. It was a big local scandal at the time. He and the other woman went to live in Portugal and, as far as I know, they're still there. The Portuguese are very keen on golf and they're great Anglophiles. Portugal is our oldest ally, did you know that?'

He had known, but he hadn't known about the rest of the story. He should have paid far more attention to Miss Butler.

He said, 'Mrs Reed has kept a great many of her husband's golfing cups. They're all polished and out on display.'

'I can understand why. It makes it easier for her to pretend that he lives there too. I met Mrs Reed once. A forceful lady, as I remember. I believe Reed tried very hard to get her to divorce him when he left her but she wouldn't. Are you looking for him on her behalf?'

'Not exactly.'

'Well, I doubt if she'll ever change her mind about a divorce. Not that it matters much these days, does it? Anything goes.'

As he left, the club secretary shook his hand. 'I hope you'll think about joining us, Colonel. You'd be very welcome. And you never know, you might enjoy it.'

He smiled and thanked him.

* * *

Joyce Reed looked surprised and not particularly pleased to see him when she opened her flat door.

'You'd better come in, Colonel.'

'Thank you.'

He stopped in front of the illuminated display cabinet. The contents glittered brightly.

'You mentioned that your husband had recently won another trophy.'

She pointed.

'That one there.'

He leaned forward to take a closer look.

She said, 'It's a very ordinary one.'

'But interesting, Mrs Reed. Unlike all the others, it has no inscription. Did you buy it yourself?'

'Why would I do that?'

'To keep up the pretence that your husband is still living with you.'

'Arthur and I have been married for more than forty years, Colonel.'

'I don't doubt that's true, Mrs Reed, but people in Frog End are wondering why they've never seen your husband. The truth is that he's never been here at all, has he? He left you some time ago. I'm sure you have your own good reasons for concealing the fact, but you'll find it difficult to do so for much longer. People are curious.'

'I do have my reasons and they're nobody else's business.'

'I'm sorry to have raised the subject.'

She shrugged her shoulders. 'It doesn't really matter now, Colonel. I'm planning to leave Frog End anyway, so you may as well know the whole sorry tale.'

'You're not obliged to tell me.'

'I know, but I will. Arthur walked out on me and went to live with a woman he'd met at the golf club in Hampshire. She was thirty-six years old, very glamorous and an excellent player. Everything I'm not. I always hoped he'd get tired of her – just like I always hoped he'd get tired of golf – but neither of those things happened and I could see they never would. We stayed legally married because I refused to consider a divorce and when the house was sold I kept all his trophies so that I could keep my pride as well. But I don't expect you to understand that.'

'As a matter of fact, I do.'

She considered him. 'You're a widower, aren't you, Colonel? I wonder which is worse to have to cope with – death or desertion?'

'I'm afraid I don't know the answer.'

'Either way, it's loss. But I think desertion is far worse. Death is seldom intentional but desertion is deliberate and total rejection. Believe me, that's very hard to live with.'

'Did Lawrence Deacon find out about your husband?'

'He certainly did. He'd known Arthur years ago before we were married and he kept making veiled remarks to me when I met him at the Manor. It was the sort of thing he liked to do – frighten and upset people – only I ignored him completely. I wasn't afraid of him, you see.'

'Do you think other people were?'

'Oh, yes. Mrs Carberry, for instance. She was terrified.'

'Why was that?'

'No idea. You'll have to ask her yourself. But I'm very glad he's dead and I can't be the only one.'

'Do you know how he was killed?'

'This is a village, Colonel. Everyone knows . . . the garden spade, the head wounds, the pools of blood. Every detail.'

'Major Cuthbertson says he saw a woman in the distance when he was at thc Manor on thc day of the murder, but she was too far away for him to identify. Could it have been you?'

'Me? The answer is definitely not, Colonel. My back was too painful to work. I stayed at home all day, resting it. I hope you're not accusing me of murdering Mr Deacon? What a preposterous idea! I couldn't even lift one of those spades off the ground, let alone batter someone to death with it.'

'I'm not accusing you of anything, Mrs Reed, but it would be useful to find out who the woman was.'

'I don't see why it need trouble you, Colonel. Inspector Squibb is in charge of the investigation, isn't he? In any case, you're barking up the wrong tree. Jacob is obviously guilty.'

'It's not obvious at all.'

'It is to me. Not that I blame Jacob. He did us all a favour, let's face it.'

She showed him to the door.

'Don't trouble to call again, Colonel. I have nothing more to say.'

'Will you be leaving soon?'

'As soon as I can sell this flat. I've never liked the place. There's something wrong about it. A bad feeling.'

He could have told her what it was – that a woman had been murdered there, not so long ago. A famous actress, past the height of her career but still beautiful. He had found her lying dead in the bath a few yards from where they were standing, killed by a switched-on electric hair dryer that had been thrown deliberately into the water. Her eyes had been wide open, looking at him in surprise and she'd had her mouth open, as though she was about to speak to him. He could have told Joyce Reed all about it, but he didn't.

'Well, I wish you the very best for the future.'

'I've enjoyed the gardening, though,' she said. 'It's done me good. I might look for somewhere with a garden next time.'

'Could I have possibly have a word with you, Colonel?'

He paused on his way out of the Hall front doorway. 'Of course, Mrs Carberry.'

She had come out of her flat and was standing halfway down the stairs. 'I won't keep you a minute.'

'I'm not in any hurry.'

'There's something else I think you should know.'

He returned to the foot of the stairs. 'Yes?'

'You asked me if Lawrence Deacon had ever upset me or been offensive and I said he hadn't. I lied to you. I'm sorry.'

He said quietly, 'We all tell lies sometimes, Mrs Carberry, myself included. What do you think I should know?'

She looked down at him, hesitating, and he could see that it was costing her dearly to tell him.

'When I was working on the herbaceous border that morning, Mr Deacon came up and grabbed hold of me. I had to fight him off and he got very angry. I'd been leading him on, he said. I'd been encouraging him all the time and now I'd suddenly changed my mind. He called me a slut and a whore and a lot of other horrible things. He said he was going to tell everyone in the village the sort of woman I really was . . . how I went after men while pretending to be an innocent widow. He'd make sure that I wouldn't be able to go on working at the Manor. Mrs Harvey wouldn't want me there once she knew the truth about me.'

'What did you do?'

'I turned my back on him and went on working. He was still saying dreadful things but, after a while, he went away. All I could think of was that I must tell Mrs Harvey and hope that she'd believe me and not him, but when I went to the stables at lunchtime she wasn't there. And later, when I was back at work, I heard the Major shouting and I ran over to the greenhouse and saw Mr Deacon's body. It was such a shock, Colonel.'

'It must have been. Did you tell Inspector Squibb about Mr Deacon's behaviour with you?'

She shook her head. 'The Inspector's the very last person I could talk to about that sort of thing. Besides, I was afraid I'd be suspected of the murder.'

'What made you decide to tell me?'

'I'd been thinking about you saying that there was no proof of Jacob's guilt and that you and Dr and Mrs Harvey believed him to be innocent. I don't know who murdered Mr Deacon, or why, Colonel, but I thought that if I told you how he behaved with me, it might help you somehow.'

'I'm very grateful, Mrs Carberry. Thank you.'

She looked at him anxiously, 'I never led him on, Colonel. Please believe me. I'm telling you the truth about that.'

'Don't worry,' he said. 'I know you are.'

The Major was counting sheep. He'd been trying to get to sleep for at least an hour while the old girl was busy driving her pigs to market alongside him. He'd prodded her several times, but it never did any good. Damn it, she was like a trooper after a night out on the tiles. Flat on her back, mouth wide open, dead to the world.

He turned over again, tugging hard at the sheets – not that it did any good either. She held on to them like a bulldog.

Fifty-one, fifty-two, fifty-three . . .

He lost count somewhere in the sixties and had to start all over again.

One, two, three, four, five . . .

He didn't know how it was with other people but his sheep were always coming through a gap in a hedge in single file, all following their leader who was obviously the only bright tool in the box. He didn't see how it would be possible to count them if they were herded together, milling around.

Twelve, thirteen, fourteen, fifteen . . .

The whisky glasses he'd bought from Seek and Find had been a big success. Even Marjorie had approved of them and so far she hadn't broken one. He'd go back and tell Claudia so, as soon as he got a chance. He wouldn't say no to another game of hide-and-seek with her.

Eighteen, nineteen, twenty, twenty-one . . .

Marjorie's pigs weren't the only thing keeping him awake. He couldn't stop thinking about the murder of Lawrence Deacon. All that blood and violence in an English country garden! You expected it in foreign countries – anywhere south of Calais – but not here, and among the tomatoes, for God's sake! He'd had a couple of bad nightmares lately and he didn't fancy having another one. Might be better to stay awake. Not that there was anything to worry about. The police had found the lunatic and got him safely behind bars. Jacob wasn't going to be coming round to Shangri-La with another spade.

Something still niggled, though. That woman he'd seen in the distance at the Manor. Just a glimpse, nothing more. She'd been there and then she was gone. The Colonel had kept asking questions about her but there'd been nothing to tell him. She'd rung a bell of some kind but that's all he could say. Damned annoying.

He stopped counting sheep and lay in the dark, eyes wide open, trying to remember. What was it about her? Think, think, think!

It came to him suddenly. He hadn't recognized her because

she'd looked quite different from how she usually looked. And now that he thought more about it, he realized who she was. Worth a mention to the Colonel in the morning, in case he was still interested, though he couldn't see how it could help.

The old girl was turning over, rolling away from him like a felled oak, which usually signalled the arrival at the market. A few last pigs were driven into the pen and there was blessed silence. The Major closed his eyes and slept.

The Colonel walked across the village green in the direction of The Close. The U-boat binoculars, reduced to their post-war landlocked role in Lupin Cottage, had, he felt sure, tracked him every step of the way.

Sheila Turner's bungalow came after Journey's End, The Nook, Tree Tops, and Shangri-La, its dullness relieved by a splendid pink pelargonium growing in a blue pot outside the front door. He knocked quietly and waited for the door to be opened.

'I wonder if I might come in for a moment, Mrs Turner?'

She stared up at him, very small and very white-faced. Skin and bone, as the Major had remarked. She looked as though the proverbial puff of wind would blow her over.

'Johnny's not here. He's at the Manor, working.'

'I know. I wanted to speak to you alone.'

'Oh . . . I see.'

He followed her into the sitting room with its cheery patterns and bright colours. 'What did you want to speak to me about, Colonel?'

'Jacob.'

'Who's he?'

'The man who works in the gardens at the Manor.'

'But I don't know anything about him.'

'He's being held by the police because they believe he murdered Lawrence Deacon. He could be tried and sent to prison for a crime he didn't commit.'

'Well, Johnny had nothing to do with it – if that's what you're thinking.'

'I'm not. I know that Johnny didn't kill Mr Deacon, but he had a lot to do with his murder.'

'What do you mean?'

'He was the reason. Your reason, Mrs Turner. The Major saw you while he was searching for a plant for his wife. You told me yourself that you'd do anything for your son. Dr and Mrs Harvey had given Johnny a lifeline, working at the Manor, and Lawrence Deacon was deliberately taking it away. You had to stop that happening.'

She rocked on her feet and the Colonel put a hand under her arm.

'Why don't you sit down?'

He sat beside her. When she started to speak again, head bent, he could scarcely hear her words.

'Johnny had been in a dark place ever since his accident . . . I thought I'd lost him forever, but when he went to work in the Manor gardens he found something to live for. I was so happy for him. I thought everything was going to be all right after all. I had this dream, you see. I was going to buy a car and learn to drive and then I was going to take Johnny anywhere he wanted to go. Just him and me. And when I told him about it, Johnny thought it was a wonderful idea. I hadn't seen him excited like that since before his accident. We got the road map out and started to look up all the places he'd like to see. We even made a long list of them. It was our secret plan.'

'It sounds a very good one.'

'But then Mr Deacon started to say horrible things to Johnny.'

'What sort of things?'

'How glad he was that Johnny would never be able to walk again. How pleased he was that he would be a cripple for the rest of his life. He told Johnny that his only son had been killed riding on the back of a motor bike but the driver, who had been his friend, had survived without a scratch. His own life had been wrecked by the loss, he said, but now, he'd be able to watch Johnny suffer, like the boy who'd killed his son should have suffered. It was justice at last, and he was going to enjoy it.'

'Did Johnny tell you what Mr Deacon had said?'

'Yes, he told me. And then he went back into his dark place. He wouldn't talk about Mr Deacon, or about the Manor gardens, or about the books that Mrs Harvey had been lending him, or about our secret plan, or about anything else to me. I'd lost him again and I didn't know what to do.'

The Colonel said quietly, 'What happened on the day that Mr Deacon died?'

Her voice sank even lower.

'I'd taken Johnny to work at the Manor and later I went back to see if I could find Mr Deacon. He was in one of the greenhouses. I begged him not to say such cruel things to Johnny and I told him the dreadful damage he'd done to him. But he didn't care. Johnny would have to get used to being a cripple, he said. He'd only himself to blame for what had happened and he'd have to pay the price for ever.'

She started to sob. The Colonel gave her his handkerchief. He waited, and after a while she went on.

When she'd left the greenhouse after pleading with Mr Deacon, Jacob had been waiting outside, she said. He had run away when he'd seen her but he had left his spade behind. She'd picked it up and gone back inside. Mr Deacon had been sitting on the stool with his back turned to her. She'd hit him over the head as hard as she could. She didn't know how many times. She couldn't remember. She didn't care. She'd done it for Johnny. She'd never meant Jacob to be blamed. It had all been for Johnny. For Johnny. For Johnny.

The Colonel put his arm around her shoulders.

FIFTEEN

'I'd never have thought her capable of it, Hugh,' Naomi said, taking a restorative swig from her glass.

'Nor would I. But pushing the wheelchair had made her very strong.'

'I didn't mean physical strength. I meant guts and nerve. Sheila always seemed such a quiet little thing. Never said boo to a goose.'

'Deacon threatened her son's chance of happiness.'

'So she let him have it with both barrels. Good for her. I might have done it myself if I'd known he was such a bastard. But what happens now?'

'The Inspector has her confession and Jacob has been released.'

'I hope Squabb was suitably grateful to you.'

'Squibb, not Squabb. No, he wasn't.'

'No surprises there. But what about Johnny? It doesn't end very well for him, does it?'

'Tom and Ruth are coming to the rescue. Tom's arranged for him to go to a special hostel and Ruth has persuaded him to carry on working at the Manor – for the time being at least. They're going to keep him under their wing.'

'You'll help him, too, won't you, Hugh?'

'In any way I can.'

'What about his poor mother?'

'I think the courts will treat her as leniently as possible.'

'Are you sure she did it, Hugh? Why weren't her fingerprints on the spade as well as Jacob's?'

'She wore gloves, Naomi. That's why. Pushing the wheelchair gave her blisters so she always kept a pair of old cotton gloves in her pocket. She told me that she put them on before she touched the spade.'

'So, she knew what she was doing. Or rather going to do.'

'She would have done anything for Johnny.'

They sat in a thoughtful silence on the terrace, watching the sun going down.

'Well, you solved the mystery in the end, Hugh.'

'No, I didn't. Freda Butler provided the essential clues, together with Tanya Carberry who told me what she knew about Deacon, and the Major finally realized that Johnny's mother was the woman he'd seen at the Manor.'

'How did he work that out?'

'He hadn't recognized her before because she had looked completely different. He'd been used to seeing her bent over the handles of the wheelchair, pushing hard. He hadn't recognized her out of context and standing upright.'

Another silence.

'The other half, Naomi?'

'I wouldn't say no.'

He re-filled their glasses.

Naomi said, 'I hear Joyce Reed's flat is up for sale. I suppose she'll move somewhere else with all the trophies and carry on pretending that the husband hasn't dumped her.'

'How did you know about that?'

'Come on, Hugh, the whole village knew! And so did you, only you've been too nice to say a word. If I could say one to her it would be not to bother any more. She's much better off without him. Or try being a widow, for a change. I can recommend it. By the way, did you know that Tanya is going off on a cruise?'

'No, I didn't.'

'Wild horses couldn't drag me near any of those ghastly boats, but apparently she and her late husband had always planned to go on one. She'll be gone for two months. All the way to Australia and all the way back again. Same people, same food, same everything. Can you imagine anything more boring? Still, maybe she'll meet a decent man. There's always the faint chance. And, speaking of chance, Hugh, did you hear the Major has won a holiday?'

Another unknown.

'No.'

'First prize in a raffle. That animal shelter thing that Freda Butler was flogging tickets for. He's won a week for two at a luxury hotel in Barcelona. I thought Marjorie would hate the whole idea and refuse to go with him, but apparently she's all in favour. Already packing her suitcase. Poor old Major! His one chance of glorious freedom gone down the plughole. Just as well, really. I'm not sure he'd know what to do with it. I see your herbs are coming along nicely, Hugh. I hope you're making good use of them.'

'When I remember.'

Naomi squinted at the pig trough. 'Room for one more, I'd say, now that you've tamed the mint. You could try tarragon. It's jolly good with chicken. Miss Jekyll's looking happy over there. You've been taking good care of her.'

'I do my best.'

'How's Thursday these days?'

'Not eating properly and getting even thinner. I'm taking him to the vet tomorrow.'

She looked thoughtfully into her glass.

'Thursday won't thank you for that, of course, Hugh, but it's the one thing you can do for him that he can't do for himself.'

'I know.'

The vet dealt expertly with Thursday's spitting, clawing fury. The Colonel listened to his calm summation of the facts and thanked him before he took his cat away. When he let Thursday out of the pet carrier into the Pond Cottage garden he stalked off in a huff.

Susan answered the phone at once.

'I was hoping it might be you, Father. Have you finished with that local problem?'

'Yes, it's been resolved.'

'Good. Then you'll be free to come and stay, like you promised?'

He said, 'I'm extremely sorry, Susan, but I can't yet.'

'Why ever not?'

'I can't leave Thursday.'

'Thursday? But I thought you'd be coming on Saturday so you can see more of Marcus.'

'I'm talking about the cat that lives with me. It's his name.'

'That mangy old stray! Why can't someone else feed him?
Or he could go into a cattery.'

'He's very ill, Susan. He's dying. I can't leave him.'

'Surely he doesn't mean more to you than your own
grandchildren, Father?'

She was upset and angry and he couldn't blame her.

'No. But I'm all he's got.'

An exasperated intake of breath.

'Well, how long is he going to take?'

'I'm afraid the vet doesn't know precisely.'

It was always hard to judge, the vet had told him. The
important thing was not to let things drag on too long. Not to
risk Thursday going off to hide up somewhere, as cats like
him, big and small, tended to do towards the end. Not to
let him suffer unnecessarily alone. The Colonel would know
when it was reaching that point and must call him. He'd come
over to Pond Cottage straight away.

After finishing the difficult conversation with his daughter-in-
law, the Colonel went out into the garden. He found Thursday
lying in the shade under the bench by the pond. The old cat
was lying stretched out on his side and lifted his head at his
approach.

The Colonel sat down and stroked him gently between
his ears.

'Hallo, old fellow. Don't worry. I won't be leaving you.'